HOW FOR A LADY

A Wetherby Brides Novel

Jerrica Knight Catania

This book is a work of fiction.
Names, characters, locations and events are either a product of the
author's imagination, fictitious or used fictitiously.
Any resemblance to any event, locale or person,
living or dead, is purely coincidental.

How to Care for a Lady
Copyright 2016 by Jerrica Knight-Catania

All rights reserved, including the right of reproduction in whole or
part in any format.
Cover by *Covers by Lily*

For Eric—
For reading every book, cover to cover.
For believing in me when I don't believe in myself.
For showing me what true love is.
I love you.

PROLOGUE

London, June 1822

There comes a time in every woman's life when she looks at her reflection in the mirror and she doesn't quite recognize herself. For Hannah Ludlum, Lady Beeston, that day was the day her husband shot her.

She clutched the cold heavy silvered mirror in her hand and stared into her tawny eyes. They were so different than they used to be. They'd once sparkled with youth and hope, but all she saw now was ten years of misery. Ten years of waiting, wanting, and hoping. She saw defeat. It stung far more than the bullet wound in her leg.

A tear eked out, and the fluttering of a sob accosted her lungs. She placed the mirror on her bedside table and lolled her head back against the pillows. What had she been thinking? Not just today. Of course it was foolish to run pell-mell across the field as her brother and husband were about to fire their pistols at one another. She'd been foolish long before then. One might have forgiven her after a year, but ten. *Ten*. How dare she hope for so long? What a waste of her precious time to spend it thinking one day, somehow, she might make her husband love her.

A bitter laugh bubbled up at the thought. Love. The only thing Beeston loved was an endless bottle of brandy and a lightskirt who would do…

Oh, blazes! She didn't even know what it was he would want the doxy to do, for heaven's sake. How about that? His own wife knew nothing about his preferences in the bedroom. After ten blasted years.

Her head began to swim, partly from her musings, but mostly from the heavy dose of laudanum the doctor had just administered. The pain in her leg had subsided quite a bit, but she grew sleepier by the moment. Which was why she was certain she was dreaming when Beeston himself walked through the door of her bedchamber. She was certain he'd disappear for a while after this morning's events. But the fact he had the bollocks to show up here sent just a tiny ray of hope to her heart.

No. She wouldn't dare. Not after last night, or this morning. She'd given him ten long years to prove that he wasn't the cruelest of men, but he'd proved to her, in no uncertain terms, he was beyond redemption. As soon as she could keep her eyes open and form a coherent sentence she would tell him so.

Her eyes were so very heavy. His form swam toward her as if the entire room had filled with water.

"Hannah," he whispered. She held her silence. "Hannah, are you sleeping, my darling?"

My darling?

"Dreaming," she mumbled. There was no other explanation for his endearment.

"The doctor said you would sleep," he continued. "But I had to see you. I had to make certain you were all right."

His voice sounded far away, and so gentle. She thought of the night they'd met. She'd spotted him across the Holifields' ballroom, but promptly lost him in the crowd, since he wasn't terribly tall, and neither was she. Her romantic younger self held onto the vision of that handsome gentleman all evening, waiting to see his face again. Wondering why she'd never seen him before, and all manner of other thoughts that flit through a young woman's head.

Warm sunlight kissed Hannah's cheeks. She tried to open her eyes, but her lids were so heavy, as if rocks lay upon them. Her mouth was dry. So dry. She shifted and a searing pain shot through her body.

"Hannah." It was Beeston. She could feel him at her side. He must have moved over her, eclipsing the sunlight, stealing the warmth, as he'd done since the day they'd said *I do*. "Can I get you something? Water? More laudanum?"

"No," she rasped. "No more."

"Water, then?"

She nodded—or at least, she thought she had. She couldn't be certain. Not until a moment later when Beeston lifted her head and pressed the edge of a glass against her lips. She drank, grateful for the cool wetness that filled her mouth and relieved her dry throat.

"Thank you," she whispered. Beeston placed the glass on the bedside table and then took her hand in his. "What are you doing here?" Hannah couldn't help but ask. It wasn't like him to be so attentive. Or to be around at all, really.

"Helping you recover." His voice wavered. "Are you in very much pain?"

Hannah managed a puff of laughter. "It feels as if Satan himself is stabbing his trident into my leg." She finally pried her eyes open to see Beeston sitting beside her, his face contorted in a mixture of horror and despair.

When had he turned so very hideous? Ten years ago, he'd been the very picture of a dashing gentleman. Light brown hair sat in gentle waves above a strong brow. Clean shaven skin. Eyes that danced with light and amusement. He'd stood with confidence, and his clothing had hugged his muscular form just so, causing every woman in the ballroom to swoon over him, in spite of his reduced stature.

"Will you ever forgive me?" he asked. It was obvious he was choking back tears.

Hannah might have felt sorry for him if she didn't find him so very pathetic. It wasn't her most charitable thought, but she was done being charitable and forgiving toward him.

"For what?" she asked, feeling stronger now, thanks to the rush of anger that surged through her. "For shooting me? Or for bedding every woman in Town? Or for forcing me into a miserable existence for the last ten years? I ought to be clear on what I'm to forgive you for."

3

If only an artist were there to capture the look upon Beeston's face, his jaw slack, his eyes filled with shock that his meek little wife had finally spoken up for herself.

"I-I—"

"The answer is no," she said, cutting him off before he attempted to come up with a pitiful excuse for his entire existence. "To everything. I do not forgive you. Not anymore."

"But you're my wife." A bit of the Beeston she knew started to creep back in—tight jaw, flaring nostrils. But she'd not be afraid of him anymore.

"Exactly. And I've been more than wifely all these ten years. You, however, have gone about your life as if I don't even exist."

Beeston only stared at her, clearly at a loss for words. She'd run out of words, herself. What was left to say? He'd treated her poorly their entire marriage, and then he'd shot her. Whether by accident or not, he'd shot her nonetheless.

"I want a divorce," she finally said, knowing full well that decision was not in her hands, nor would it ever be. If she were to obtain a divorce, it would have to be at Beeston's request. He didn't look terribly amenable to the idea.

"A divorce?" he practically roared. "How dare you? You carry my *child*."

Oh, right. There was that. Not that she actually carried his child, but that she'd told him she did. Bugger. She'd have to come clean, which would further enrage him, but at least they were in her brother's house. If Beeston attempted any bodily harm to her, someone would come rushing to her aid.

She swallowed over the hard lump in her throat. "I lied." Best to state it as simply as possible.

Beeston's eyes knit together in a frown. "I beg your pardon?" His voice was quiet, dangerous. It made Hannah's hands tremble.

But she wouldn't let him get the best of her. If she was ever going to stand up to him, this was the time to do it, while she was already injured and in a great deal of pain. How much more damage could he inflict? He could murder her, but part of Hannah wondered if that wouldn't be preferable to a lifetime spent as his wife.

Hannah lolled her head back against the fluffy pillows, growing ever more weary. "I said, I lied. I was never *enceinte*. I only said that because…because…"

"Because why?" he roared, clearly impatient to know why she would do such a thing.

"Because I thought it would make you love me." The words were out before she could stop them. They sounded so foolish when she spoke them aloud. What a silly fool she was. Beeston loved no one but himself, and an unborn child wouldn't change that.

Tears tried to push their way from behind her eyelids, but she wouldn't allow it. Not now. Not in front of him. She would suffer in silence, as she always had.

When she'd gained her composure, she dared to meet his eyes. He sat stone still, staring at her, his jaw set, his brow furrowed. Was he angry? Sad? She couldn't tell. This man she'd been married to for ten long years was impossible for her to read. She knew nothing about him, save the rumors she'd heard of his dalliances and drunken nights at the seediest of London's establishments. She knew the money she'd brought to the marriage was long gone, and there was little left in their coffers.

After an excruciatingly long moment, Beeston rose from his chair and walked silently to the door. Without another word, he quit the room.

ONE

London, July 1822

Dr. Graham Alcott sat with a brandy in one hand, a medical essay in the other, his feet propped upon a cushioned footstool. He wore his grey satin dressing gown and the pair of slippers his sister had given him for his birthday. His belly was well satisfied, after a meal of soup and bread, and he savored the silence of his rented rooms in Marylebone.

This was no different from any other night of his existence since he'd moved to London six years ago. Occasionally, the monotony was broken up with dinners at his sister's home or a drink with his brother-in-law at the club, when they were in Town. But Graham wasn't much for social gatherings. He preferred to keep to himself, in the company of his books. Always medical books, for he had quite an obsession with healing the sick.

No. Not just healing them. Finding new and *better* ways to heal them. Ways beyond the ken of his superiors. Not that he didn't respect the surgeons and physicians who had come before him. Surely, they were doing their best. Yet watching them bleed patients nearly to death with the use of medieval contraptions or, God forbid, leeches, had sent Graham looking for alternatives.

Of course, he'd watched his father do the same, and he'd resorted to such measures on occasion when he doctored in his hometown of Ravenglass. But he'd always hated it. Always wondered if there was another way. Even now, his eyes scanned over an essay by a leading doctor from Edinburgh who offered many alternatives to bloodletting.

"I'm sorry to bother you, Dr. Alcott."

Graham turned to find his valet standing in the doorway of the small parlor. "What is it, Dorian?"

"You have a visitor."

"At this hour?"

"Dr. Pritchard would like to have a moment."

Of course. Dr. Pritchard. His mentor, his sponsor. The man who had seen to his advancement from Country Doctor to a genuine doctor, worthy of his title. "Do let him in."

Dorian disappeared and returned a moment later, Dr. Pritchard on his heels. Graham rose from his comfortable chair to greet the older man, more than a bit curious to know what this late-night meeting was all about.

"Dr. Alcott, I do hope you'll forgive the intrusion. I see you were preparing for bed."

"Not at all," Graham said, guiding the other doctor to a nearby chair. "Brandy?"

Dr. Pritchard shook his head and held up a hand. "No, no. I've only come to ask you a favor."

"A favor?"

"I've been summoned to care for the Countess of Kilworth through the remainder of her pregnancy. She's had a rough go of it, and the earl doesn't want to take any chances."

"Understandably."

"This means, though, that I must refer all my patients to someone I trust."

Graham couldn't stop the smile that came to his lips. "I'm honored."

"Only…I can't trust them all to you."

The smile fell quickly from Graham's lips. "I beg your pardon?" Why was the old man here then?

"Dr. Alcott, I need you to care for one patient in particular, actually."

Well, that was a surprise. "Just one?"

"She's a widow who has suffered a great deal, though all you need to know is that she's been shot in the leg. I've cared for her to the best of my abilities, but I think she would quite benefit from your…" He glanced at the essay that lay on the side table and took a steadying breath. "Unorthodox ways."

7

A small grin broke out on Graham's lips. "Just because they are *new* does not mean they are unorthodox."

"So you say." He leaned back in his chair. "They will pay you handsomely to see to her every need."

"I am not interested in money."

Dr. Pritchard shook his head. "You young revolutionaries."

"My beliefs are quite Quakerish, actually."

"Yes, but one who is out to change the world."

Graham shrugged. It wasn't untrue. "Who will see to your other patients?"

"I've a few colleagues who are willing, but those who are most important, well...the two of us shall see to them."

"Is all human life not important?"

Dr. Pritchard shook his head. "Not to the *ton*."

Graham couldn't argue that point. He himself might be considered the dung on their shoe if they weren't in need of medical attention. "When do I meet my new patient?"

"Tomorrow. First thing."

It wasn't exactly what Graham wished to be doing with his life, though he had to admit, if he had only one patient to care for, and a great sum of money filling his pockets, he might very well be able to devote the rest of his time to more research. The more he thought about it, the more he wondered why he was hesitating.

"I'll admit, I'm not entirely certain of this path, but...I quite owe you my life, and if you need me, Dr. Pritchard, then who am I to refuse you?"

~*~

A knock came at Hannah's door just as she took the last bite of her breakfast. "Enter," she called with a full mouth of egg, and then promptly swallowed before her friendly old doctor poked his head in. Hannah smiled sweetly at him.

"Dr. Pritchard!" she greeted him. "Do come in."

"Good morning, my lady," he said, and then turned to look at something in the hall. "I've actually brought someone with me, if you'd be willing to permit him entry as well."

"Of course." Hannah set her tray aside and sat up a little straighter as Dr. Pritchard stepped into the room and held the door open for whoever it was he'd brought along.

In the next moment, a tall, slender man stepped over the threshold, nearly sucking all the air from the room at the same time. Or perhaps just sucking the air from Hannah's lungs, since Dr. Pritchard seemed quite unaffected. Blazes. This stranger was quite handsome, and Hannah wished more than anything that she hadn't been confined to a bed for the last six weeks with only sponge baths to clean herself. Her hair must look a fright, and her pallor ghostly.

She fidgeted nervously, tucking her hair behind her ear, and then untucking it again, wondering which way might cast her in the best light.

"Lady Beeston, may I present Dr. Alcott."

The handsome doctor dipped his head, causing a lock of his dark hair to fall over his forehead. When he lifted his head again, he wore a wide smile on his lips. One that made Hannah's heart skip more than one beat.

"A pleasure, Dr. Alcott," she said, trying to keep her wits about her. "What a lucky girl I must be to have not one but *two* doctors attend to me."

Dr. Pritchard cleared his throat and stepped forward. "I'm afraid you shall still only have one doctor attending you, my lady. Dr. Alcott will see to your recovery from now on."

In spite of her initial attraction to the young physician, this news came as quite a shock and a great disappointment. Hannah couldn't seem to form a terribly polite question in her mind, so she blurted out, "But where are you going?" in what was most certainly a panicked, childish tone.

Dr. Pritchard gave a little laugh. "I'm afraid the Earl of Kilworth has paid for my exclusive services. His wife is having a rather difficult time with her pregnancy, so I will attend her at their country estate until the baby is born."

"Oh." Hannah couldn't ignore the wash of uneasiness that came over her at the mention of a pregnant woman. Or was it jealousy? Ten years married to Beeston had not yielded a single pregnancy, and now she was thirty, and widowed, and unable to even walk, let alone attend a ball where she might meet a man willing to take a chance on a woman well past her prime who walked with a limp. "Well, I shall certainly miss your smiling face, Dr. Pritchard. You've been quite a comfort to me these past six weeks."

A sadness washed over the man's wrinkled face, and he came to sit on the edge of her bed. He took Hannah's hand in his — a gesture that brought tears to her eyes immediately. "You are a strong and brave woman, my lady. You shall be just fine. And I promise Dr. Alcott is every bit as qualified to care for you as I, perhaps even more so." He patted the back of her hand and then stood again. "I have told him all he needs to know about your situation." He gave her a knowing look. "Whether or not you share the rest is entirely up to you."

Hannah nodded and swiped an errant tear from her cheek. So, he'd told him about the shooting, but not about Beeston's decision to take his own life. She actually wished he *had* told him. It wasn't a memory she liked to relive, not since the catalyst for his actions had been her asking for a divorce.

"Thank you, Dr. Pritchard," she said.

Dr. Pritchard smiled. "Goodbye, Lady Beeston."

~*~

Graham had not been expecting this. And by *this* he meant a lovely, kind-hearted patient, still fairly young in years, with eyes the color of cinnamon. When Dr. Pritchard had spoken of a widow with a difficult past, he'd imagined an old woman, sad and hardened by life. He couldn't have been more wrong.

The door clicked shut behind him, leaving Graham alone with his new patient. She fidgeted with her mahogany hair, trying to keep the pieces in place to no avail. They were shiny and matted — clearly she'd not enjoyed a proper bath in quite a while.

"Ahem." She cleared her throat, and then finally met his eyes. "Do you...do you need to...*examine* me?"

Graham only barely held back the chuckle that rose to his throat. But it wouldn't be in good taste to laugh at her uneasiness. His goal with her, as with all his patients, was to put her at ease.

"Eventually," he said, striding nearer the bed and placing his black leather bag beside the chair. "May I sit?" Lady Beeston nodded; he sat. "I know this is rather abrupt, this change. I'm happy to simply get to know you for today, and tomorrow we will start the treatment."

"Treatment?" The widow's eyes grew round, and her lips pinched together like a tiny, pink rosebud.

Graham cocked his head. "Might I ask what kind of regimen Dr. Pritchard had you on?"

She blinked several times. "I don't know if one could call it a regimen," she said with a little shrug. "My sister-in-law has been ordered to change my bandages every few days now. Laudanum for the pain, of course. Bed rest, which is perhaps the worst of all."

It wasn't surprising the old doctor had her on a traditional path of recovery, but new things were being discovered in medicine every day, and Lady Beeston would be his first test subject.

"Why no bath?" he asked, causing her cheeks to turn a wild shade of red.

She shrugged again — clearly a nervous tick of hers. "Dr. Pritchard worried it would cause infection in the wound," she explained and then cleared her throat. "I asked more than once."

A smile spread Graham's lips wide. "You needn't be embarrassed. I've smelled far worse than you."

11

The baroness stared at him aghast, her jaw unhinged, but clearly at a loss for words. He'd just called her smelly, after all, but only in jest. Did she have a sense of humor?

Another moment passed before the barest of smiles twitched the corners of her mouth upward. "Well, I suppose that ought to make me feel better." A little snort escaped her nose, and then they both started to laugh. Not an uproarious kind of laugh, but the kind that sliced through the palpable tension in the room, like a knife through butter.

"Well, you shall have something to look forward to now," he said. "Tomorrow, you shall take a bath."

"Forgive me if I can't stop smiling, Doctor. This is most welcome news."

He wanted to tell her that he never wanted her to stop smiling, for it was a smile that lit up the room. But that would be rather unprofessional of him, so he simply said, "I'm glad of that, my lady. Now, if you're comfortable with it, I'd like to examine your wound."

She clamped her pink lips together, eclipsing her smile, and nodded. Her eyelids fluttered, as if nerves might be getting the better of her.

"If it's too soon—"

"It's not!" she shouted. "Truly. Please, proceed."

TWO

He was a doctor. Surely, he'd seen plenty of bare legs in his practice. And a leg was a leg, was it not? There was nothing for her to be nervous about. The fact that he was so very handsome and charming and currently pushing her dress up beyond where propriety would allow was irrelevant to the fact he was a *doctor*. He was merely doing his job.

So why was her heart racing at such an alarming rate?

She watched as he lifted her dress ever higher, until it practically revealed her nether regions. Blast. Why couldn't Beeston have shot her lower down on her leg? Why did it have to be so very high? It was one thing for Dr. Pritchard to examine her and tend to her wound. He was old and unattractive and married. He'd delivered hundreds of babies. There was no need to feel modest before him. But Dr. Alcott...

"How many babies have you delivered?" Hannah blurted out before she could stop herself.

Dr. Alcott's hands paused, resting on her thigh, near the wound. He looked up at her, his eyes piercing, causing her heart to race even faster than it had been before. At least if one was going to have an attack of the heart it was best to have one with a doctor present.

"I beg your pardon?" he asked.

"Babies. Have you delivered any?" Hannah was rather surprised at her own bluntness. She was normally one to beat about the bush or cushion her words with gentle phrases such as, "If you don't mind sharing," or "Pardon my candidness." It seemed her mouth was running away with her today, and she couldn't exactly explain why. Something about this man...

Dr. Alcott sat back and pulled his hands away from her leg. Oddly enough, this made Hannah even more nervous. She felt so exposed and was acutely aware of the slightly chilly air that breezed over her skin. Skin that should most certainly be covered in the presence of a man.

"Does it make any difference?" he asked.

"No," Hannah answered, and then questioned why she was lying. "Yes," she amended. "I mean...a little."

A smile crossed his thin lips as he reached into his bag to retrieve a small bottle of something—a salve for her leg, perhaps.

"I was the only doctor in my small town in Cumberland, so yes, I have seen my share of babies into this world." He narrowed his eyes on her. "Does that make you feel better?"

She thought it should have, but it didn't. It was still unnerving to have him starting at her bare leg.

"Why did you leave Cumberland?" she asked, desperate to evade his question.

"Oh, I left years ago, when I was presented with the opportunity to apprentice with Dr. Pritchard. That, combined with my sister marrying a Londoner, brought me here." He focused on the wound. "Is it sore to the touch?"

Hannah nodded.

"I will be as gentle as I can."

Hannah sucked in a sharp breath as he pressed his hand against her wound. It was sore and uncomfortable, but she fought to maintain her composure. It was silly, really. She'd done the same with Dr. Pritchard. For some odd reason, she was afraid of offending them or hurting their feelings should she complain too much about their administrations being too painful to endure.

"I'm sorry," he muttered, his tone low and genuine, reverberating through Hannah's body, and taking away all thoughts of discomfort. "I know how painful that is."

"You do?" She was intrigued. Had he suffered his own gunshot wound before? Perhaps a lesion from sword fighting? Was it over a woman?

"I do," he said, placing a fresh bandage over her leg. "Dog bite."

Well, that wasn't terribly romantic as far as wounds went, but she was still curious as to how he'd come to the dog bite. "Your own dog?"

He shook his perfect head of dark hair. "A patient, actually."

"You mean the *dog* of a patient."

"No. I mean a patient." His lips stretched over an expanse of lovely, white teeth, which twinkled almost as much as his dark eyes did. "My practice in Cumberland extended to animals as well."

Hannah unsuccessfully tried to stifle a laugh. It came out as more of a snort. "I'm sorry," she said, trying to sober herself. "I don't mean to laugh."

"You needn't apologize. It does seem preposterous to me, too. Thankfully, things have progressed since my departure. They have both a human doctor *and* an animal doctor in Ravenglass now."

"Ravenglass?" That name sounded familiar. "Where have I heard that name before?"

"Perhaps you're familiar with Marisdùn Castle," he ventured.

That was it. "The haunted Marisdùn Castle?"

Dr. Alcott nodded. "The very one. Perhaps you can convince my sister to tell you of her own personal involvement with one of the ghosts there sometime."

Hannah swallowed hard. It was quite presumptuous to infer she'd meet his sister one day. But it made her feel warm all over. "And what about you? Have you ever encountered a ghost?"

For the first time since he'd walked into her chamber, Dr. Alcott's confidence seemed to waver. "Lady Beeston, I have seen death more times than I'd care to count. It would be odd if I *hadn't* encountered a ghost."

"That must be difficult. Seeing death so often, I mean."

15

He shrugged. "Comes with the territory, I suppose. Though I much prefer the experimental side of medicine. Trying to save lives with new techniques and such."

"Which is why you don't agree with Dr. Pritchard's regimen for me."

A smile crossed his lips. "Did I say that?"

"You didn't have to."

He pulled her dress back down over her legs. Hannah had almost forgotten she was so exposed for a moment. "What do we do now?"

"Now...we walk."

~*~

The look on Lady Beeston's face spoke volumes in regard to how she felt about taking a walk. Dr. Pritchard had confined her to her bed all this time, but she was never going to get better if she didn't exercise the leg.

"But my leg," she stammered. "What if...what if..."

"What if what?" Graham pressed. "The only risk to your leg right now is weakness of the muscles. Soon, you won't be able to use your leg at all, if you don't start exercising it immediately."

"Does Dr. Pritchard know about this?"

"I'm afraid Dr. Pritchard is overly concerned with other factors, such as over exertion, fever, infection. Things we needn't worry about now. Your wound is healing as it should, if not quickly enough, and..." He placed a hand to her forehead. It was soft and lovely, and he had to fight the urge to run his fingers through her chestnut hair, dirty as it might have been. "Your temperature is completely normal."

A slight smile broke out on her lips. They formed the most perfect Cupid's bow on the top, and a plump little pout on the bottom. "Well, then. I suppose I'm ready for a walk."

Graham was still reeling from seeing her lovely leg exposed to him for such an extended about of time. It wasn't professional of him to have such thoughts about a patient, but blast if it wasn't the most delicately rounded leg he'd ever seen. Never mind she hadn't used it in weeks, or that it had a puckered, purple gun wound near the top of it—it was still lovely enough to set his blood racing through his veins.

"Yes, I suppose you are," he managed. "Allow me to help you to your feet."

She reached out a hand, which he took, while placing an arm around her slender waist. He hated to hear her wince—after six weeks, her recovery ought to be further along—but hopefully his methods would speed the healing more so than those of Dr. Pritchard.

"I'm sorry," he murmured in response to her groan as he lifted her to a standing position. "Breathe. Deeply. There's no rush."

"I'm seeing spots," she said, wilting just a bit in his arms.

"It will be all right. I'm here. I have you."

THREE

Setting aside the fact that she was nearly blinded with pain, Hannah couldn't help but be warmed by the doctor's gentle manner. Her husband had never shown her any such kindness. Of course, it crossed her mind that he was only doing his duty as her physician, but then...Dr. Pritchard was never quite so gentle or caring. Dr. Pritchard had certainly never inspired such longing in her heart.

Hannah had to take a moment and remind herself that she'd been starved of love for far too long. That her reaction to this man—her *doctor*—was merely because she'd been deprived of attention for...well, forever, it seemed. If she wasn't careful, she'd make things awkward between them. Something she most certainly didn't want. He promised to make her well—to allow her walk again—she wouldn't scare him off by falling in love with him.

She laughed inwardly at the idea. In love. She'd known him the lesser part of an hour. What a preposterous thought.

"How are you feeling now?" came his velvety voice, so close to her ear, it sent a shiver down her spine.

The spots were gone from her vision, and the sharpness of the pain had subsided to a dull throb. "I think I'm ready to proceed."

"We won't go far," he promised, and then he tightened his grip around her lower back, as she braced a hand in his. "Small steps."

It took so much of her effort to concentrate on trying to walk that she barely registered how strong his arms were. But only barely. He seemed so lean when one simply gazed upon him, but to have that band of steel around her back, that unwavering arm supporting her, it was enough to make a lady swoon. Especially one that was already in a great deal of pain and discomfort.

"So, what have you been doing these six weeks, holed away in your chamber?" Dr. Alcott asked as they inched along.

Hannah sighed. "A great deal of reading," she began. "My sister-in-law visits me often to share tales of the outside world. Mother drops in occasionally, but..."

"And your brother?" he prompted, clearly sensing the topic of Mother was not a pleasant one.

"Oh, yes. He visits too." A little smile crossed her lips. "He sneaks me a little brandy from time-to-time as well."

Dr. Alcott threw his head back and gave a hearty laugh. "Well, then it hasn't been all bad, has it?"

"I'll admit I've acquired a taste for the stuff. My late husband never would have approved, though Heaven knows he was more often in his cups than out of them." Speaking of Beeston always set her nerves on edge, and she found herself needing a deep breath to steady herself.

"My professional opinion is that a nip of the spirits is good for the mind and the body every now and again, be ye male or female. You needn't worry about being judged by me."

Hannah looked up at him. "I never was." It seemed a ridiculous thing to say, since she'd known him all of a half hour, but it was true. She just knew, in her heart, that he was a different kind of doctor. A different kind of man.

He didn't respond, but the barest of grins tipped the edges of his lips up. "Look, my lady."

Hannah followed his gaze and realized they'd reached the edge of the stairs at the end of the corridor. She hadn't even noticed how far they'd come.

"How do you feel?" he asked.

Truth be known, she was a little light-headed, though she was starting to question whether it was the walk or the company. "I feel...happy," she said. "I was beginning to wonder if I'd ever leave the bed, let alone walk down the corridor."

"What the devil is this?"

The stern voice startled both of them, and Hannah craned her head around to find her brother practically stomping toward them. His dark curls shook with every step, and his blue eyes were narrowed upon Dr. Alcott.

"Dr. Alcott," Hannah said calmly, for she had dealt with her brother and his temper often enough to know he was more bark than he was bite. "May I introduce my brother, the Duke of Somerset. Evan, this is Dr. Alcott."

Evan approached, and Hannah had to laugh. As tall as her brother was, the doctor still towered over him. Goodness, he was tall.

"Your Grace," Dr. Alcott said, bending his head in deference.

Evan wasn't nearly as polite. "Where is Dr. Pritchard?"

"He's gone to care for the Countess of Kilworth through the rest of her confinement. Dr. Alcott will care for me in his absence."

"But why the devil are you out of bed?" he asked, and then realized he ought to direct the question to the doctor directly. "Why the devil is she out of bed?"

"I realize you are more accustomed to Dr. Pritchard's methods, but I assure you, your sister will come to no harm."

"He says it will advance my healing," Hannah put in, eager to put her brother at ease.

"And what credentials do you have?"

"Goodness, Evan," Hannah said. "He is a doctor, is he not? That alone speaks to his credentials."

"It is quite all right," Dr. Alcott rushed to reassure Hannah. "Your Grace, I would be happy to discuss my training and history with you, but this is unfortunately not a good time to do that. It is important to see your sister back to her bed before we overtax her."

Evan's jaw twitched just a bit, but he nodded and backed away, so Hannah and the doctor could make their way back to her bedchamber.

HOW TO CARE FOR A LADY

~*~

Graham sat in the burgundy leather chair, facing His Grace, the Duke of Somerset. Someone of Graham's status ought to have been intimidated by someone of the duke's status, but Graham had dealt with many a titled gentlemen, and had learned that with a title came a great deal of entitlement. The best way to deal with men of his kind was to allow them to think his treatments—his "new way" of thinking—were their idea.

The duke gave a tight smile and drummed his fingers on the mahogany desk. "I apologize if I came off rather brutish before," he began. "It has been quite…unsettling, these events of the past six weeks or so. If it weren't for my new wife, I'd have gone mad already."

"I know only a bit of the story, but I can deduce that you all have been through a rather trying time."

The duke leaned forward. "To be truthful, we're all quite pleased that the baron decided to end his own life. Bunny will be better off for it."

Graham struggled to get over the shock of the duke's words and tried to focus instead on who the hell Bunny might be. "Bunny?"

"My sister. Lady Beeston," the duke clarified. "Forgive me. It's what I've always called her, and it's hard to break old habits."

"Of course," Graham said, at a loss for anything else to say.

"So, go on. Tell me what I wish to know about you. Dr. Pritchard has been my family's doctor for decades—I knew all I needed to know of him."

"I understand," Graham began. "I know it must be unsettling to find a new doctor caring for your sister, but I assure you, I am qualified and I will see to her full recovery."

Somerset's eyes rounded below raised eyebrows. "*Full* recovery? Don't you think that's a bit optimistic? Dr. Pritchard said she'd be lucky to ever walk again at all."

"And yet, there she was, walking the halls of your home with me just a few minutes ago."

The duke narrowed his ice blue eyes on him. "I don't know whether I'm annoyed by your arrogance, or impressed by it."

Graham had to admit that stung a bit. He wasn't trying to be arrogant, just confident. "I don't mean to put you off, Your Grace," he said, changing his tone. "But there is no reason your sister shouldn't make a full recovery, regardless of what Dr. Pritchard said."

Eyes still narrowed, the duke nodded. "Go on," he said, his tone a challenge.

Graham scooted to the edge of his chair, his passion on the subject forcing him forward, igniting that familiar fire in his belly. "You see, Dr. Pritchard is of the old school of thought."

"The old school?"

"But there is a *new* thought to be found on almost every topic of medicine. Why, just the other day I read about alternatives to laudanum for easing pain. Things that have been used for centuries in China and India—"

"China? *India?*" The duke threw back his head and laughed, though it was hollow, devoid of any real mirth at all. "Surely you jest! You can't possibly think remedies from a primitive and barbaric world are better than what the English have discovered."

Graham should have known he'd be laughed at. Men of the duke's ilk found it hard to stray from tradition. But he'd not be thwarted. Lady Beeston *would* walk again, if not run. "The true barbarism is in the English methods, Your Grace. Bloodletting will be a thing of the past soon, I assure you."

"But I've seen with my own eyes how it heals."

"And I have seen how it kills."

Silence fell over the room, save a little bird chirping a high-pitched tune just outside the study window. The duke narrowed his eyes on him.

"Perhaps I should look for another doctor. As much as I respect Dr. Pritchard and his opinion, I fear his judgment has failed me in this regard."

Graham hadn't been expecting that. He'd not even thought about the fact the duke had the power to dismiss him, but of course that was foolish. He was probably the one paying for his services—he could dismiss him without another thought. But Graham wasn't going to let that happen.

"Perhaps we can come to a...compromise." He practically choked on the word. He hated to kowtow to someone who knew nothing of medicine, but sometimes one had to swallow their pride for the greater good.

His Grace leaned back in his chair and nonchalantly lifted his ankle to rest on the opposite knee. "Go on."

"I can continue some of Dr. Pritchard's work," he said slowly, trying to come up with a plan that wouldn't completely compromise his integrity. "While gently integrating some newer methods."

"In my experience, it is hard to mix the old with the new."

"There's no reason the methods cannot work hand-in-hand." Truthfully, he didn't know if that was true. How could he keep her abed *and* encourage her to walk at the same time? But he would say whatever he had to say to set the duke at ease.

Somerset leaned forward and placed his elbows on the dark, mahogany desk, his icy blue eyes fixed so intently on Graham that he began to sweat a bit beneath his starched collar. "If any harm comes to my sister, I shall make certain you are never able to practice medicine in this city again. Is that clear?"

Graham swallowed over the lump in his throat, trying to keep calm and confident in the face of the brooding duke, in spite of the fact he felt as if he might toss up his accounts. Or cry. Or both. He wasn't usually a cowering man, but for some odd reason, the stakes felt high in this particular situation.

"Perfectly," he finally managed.

"I will be watching you," the duke added, as if it were necessary.

"I would expect nothing less." There was sarcasm in his words, but if the duke noticed, he didn't say as much.

Graham took himself from the study, breathing in the taste of freedom as he entered the corridor. A million thoughts ran through his mind in light of the days' events. Part of him wanted to run home to Ravenglass and leave this harsh city behind. He'd kept himself nicely cocooned for the past six years, shadowing Dr. Pritchard and spending time only with those who made him feel comfortable. And now he was decidedly outside his realm of comfort.

Yet, something was keeping him from running away or from even standing up to the duke. No, not something. Someone.

Lady Beeston needed his help—she needed hope, wanted it, even. He could see it in her eyes, so full of sadness and regret. Graham could only imagine what she'd been through. A widow with a gunshot wound. What in the world had happened there? And were the two related?

A door creaked somewhere nearby, bringing Graham back to his senses. He'd been standing lamely in the corridor just outside the duke's study—how awkward that would have been if Somerset had found him there.

He headed for the front door, gathered his things from the butler, and set off for his rented rooms. He was expected at his sister's for dinner that evening—perhaps she could shed some light on the tale of Lady Beeston.

FOUR

Hannah opened her eyes, taking a moment to orient herself. In a whoosh, the pain came flooding back, and only when she winced did her sister-in-law say anything.

"You're awake!" Grace said, startling Hannah.

"Goodness, Grace," she said, trying to breathe deeply through the pain. "I didn't even realize you were here."

"I was waiting for you to wake up."

"Surely, you have better things to do with your time than watch me sleep."

"I was *reading,* thank you very much," she retorted. "But I had to tell you what I heard this afternoon."

Hannah pushed herself up to a sitting position as the pain subsided to a dull throb, which she'd become quite used to now. "Don't tell me you were eavesdropping again."

Grace tossed her blonde curls over her shoulder and said haughtily, "Of course I was. Just because I'm a duchess now doesn't mean they tell me everything. I'm still forced to find things out on my own from time to time."

Hannah grinned at her sister-in-law. "Well, then, go on, before it eats you up inside. I know how difficult it is for you to keep a secret."

"Evan really took your new doctor to task this afternoon."

"Well, I knew he would. If Dr. Alcott hadn't been holding me, I think Evan might have shoved him down the stairs. Do say he didn't release him of his duties."

"Dr. Alcott just barely survived. He agreed to compromise."

"Compromise? I'm more surprised to hear that *Evan* agreed to compromise."

Grace flashed her enigmatic smile. "Well, he is slightly less rigid since I came along, don't you think?"

"Slightly," Hannah replied with a wink. The truth was, her brother had been quite troubled when he'd returned from France, brooding and angry, yet still her champion. Always her champion. Now they both had a champion in Grace—she was quite a wonderful addition to their family. She'd brought levity and light to an altogether darkened family. Of course, Mother was still...Mother. But even she had softened a bit since Grace's arrival in their lives. "But go on...tell me about this compromise."

Grace shrugged her slight shoulders. "There isn't much to tell. After much arguing about whether the English methods were more barbaric than those of the Chinese or Indians, Dr. Alcott finally asked for the compromise. I can only imagine he feared being let go. But now he must fear his reputation."

"Why is that?"

"Because Evan told him if any harm came to you, he'd make certain he never practiced medicine in London again."

Hannah rolled her eyes. "Oh, Evan!"

"Truly. Poor Dr. Alcott. When he left the study, he stood in the hallway for at least two full minutes. Just standing there with a sort of dumbfounded look on his face."

"Evan has that effect on people." Hannah shook her head and tsked. "I do wish he would leave people be sometimes."

"I can't imagine that ever happening, but we can hope, can't we?"

They both giggled at that, and then Grace asked, "Are you comfortable?"

Hannah took a deep breath, assessing her comfort level. "Actually," she said, "I am. I do think the throbbing has subsided. Goodness, it was good to be out of this bed," she went on. "If Evan doesn't approve of me walking about, I may have to employ you to distract him when Dr. Alcott comes calling."

"Oh, if there's one thing I know how to do, it's to distract my husband."

Heat infused Hannah's cheeks. It always did when Grace spoke so openly about her relations with Evan. Really, Hannah didn't need to know about their private affairs, but it seemed Grace often forgot that Evan was her brother. "Well, thank you," she managed. "I think I ought to rest now."

"Of course. I'll come see you later on."

Grace left the room, and Hannah nestled back into her covers. But she couldn't sleep, not without her laudanum. She stared at the tiny bottle on her nightstand, wanting it and wanting to toss it out at the same time. She'd been dependent on a cold, distant man for so long, and now she was becoming dependent on something equally as cold and distant. It would never warm her as she wanted to be warmed. It would never hold her or whisper sweet nothings in her ear or tell her it loved her. No, it would just make her forget how much she longed for those things. And that was enough to make her reach over, take hold of the bottle, and administer another dose.

~*~

"Well, well, well, the good doctor has decided to join us tonight"

Graham sauntered across the drawing room of his sister's town home toward his brother-in-law, Viscount Wolverly—better known as Wolf to his friends—who stood at the side bar, pouring a tumbler full of Graham's favorite brandy.

"I had a feeling you might bring out the good stuff this evening," Graham said with a smirk for the viscount.

They shook hands, and then Graham gladly accepted the beverage before taking a sip of its spicy goodness. "Where's Daphne? I expected to find her here with you."

Wolf tossed his head toward the door—or somewhere beyond, perhaps. "In the kitchen. Where else?"

"Ah," Graham nodded. "Then I suspect our dessert will be accompanied by rum butter, then?"

"Isn't it always?"

"Touché." Graham's sister, Daphne, though a viscountess now, couldn't seem to quite let go of her old profession as a purveyor of Cumberland rum butter. To be truthful, no one made it like she did, so Graham wasn't complaining. "And what of my niece and nephew?"

"With their mother. Driving Cook mad, but Daphne insists that if they want to learn the art of making rum butter, they shall be permitted."

"You can take the girl out of Cumberland..."

"Indeed." Wolf gestured to the door. "Ah, here they are now!"

"A little bit messy," Daphne said, ambling into the room with her two young children hanging onto her skirts. "But here, nonetheless."

She crossed the room and kissed Graham on the cheek. "You smell delicious," he said, and then he turned to his tiny niece. "Why, I could just gobble you all up!" He scooped little Daisy into his arms and pretended to gnaw at her blonde ringlets while she giggled unabashedly.

"Uncle, stop!" she squealed while her older brother jumped up and down, shouting, "Me! Me!"

"Oh, you want to be gobbled too?" he called as he set Daisy on her feet again and then scooped Marcus into his arms to repeat the game.

"All right, that's enough," Daphne finally declared, her tone laced with both laughter and exhaustion. "Nanny is here to take you to the nursery."

Nanny stood in the doorway, a genteel woman of approximately forty years old, her hands folded primly in front of her and a serene smile on her lips. Both children groused at having to go to bed, but after kisses for their parents and their uncle, they followed Nanny out the door.

"Claret, my love?" Wolf asked, holding out a small glass of the dark red wine.

"Please!" Daphne grabbed at the glass as if it held all the answers to her problems and swallowed down a large and unladylike gulp.

"Was it that bad below stairs?" Graham laughed.

"Worse!" Daphne said, plopping onto the chintz settee. "If it's not the children making a racket, then it's Cook shouting about how we're destroying her kitchen. It was much easier in Ravenglass."

"To Cook's credit, the aristocracy don't typically prepare their own food," Wolf put in, relaxing into his own seat across from Daphne.

Daphne only shook her head, and then turned to Graham. "Sit down, won't you? Have you any news to share? Goodness, I'm desperate to talk about anything that doesn't pertain to dolls or sword fights or the general bickering of two tiny terrors."

"You don't *have* to allow them in the kitchen, you know?" Wolf interrupted before Graham could get a word out.

"Oh, hush. You know this discussion is futile."

"And yet she will continue to complain," Wolf said to Graham.

Some might be uncomfortable with spousal arguments, but Graham was quite used to Wolf and Daphne's arguing. They did it often enough, in spite of the fact they adored one another.

"Ignore him," Daphne said as Graham took his seat. "Tell us what is new in the world of medicine."

Daphne had always taken an interest in Graham's studies and profession. Their father had been the town doctor in Ravenglass, before he and Mother had perished in a fire. That was how Graham had ended up the local doctor and eventually secured an apprenticeship in London. "A great deal, actually, but even more exciting is that Dr. Pritchard is headed to the country."

Both Daphne and Wolf furrowed their brows.

"Why is that exciting?" Daphne wondered.

"Because he's left a very wealthy patient in my hands."

Whatever exhaustion had plagued Daphne moments ago seemed to disappear. She jumped to the edge of her seat. "Oh, you must tell me who it is!"

Graham laughed. "I knew you'd be excited. But I must ask for your discretion in the matter. Both of you."

"My lips are sealed. Now go on," she urged him.

Graham looked to Wolf, who nodded his agreement, and then back to his sister who was practically salivating at the mouth. "The Duke of Somerset has brought me on—"

"To care for his sister!"

So she did know about her. He nodded. "Lady Beeston is still not recovered from her situation."

"I can't imagine anyone would be," Daphne put in, her eyes turning sad. "Poor dear has apparently been through quite an ordeal."

"You know her?"

Daphne shook her blonde head. "We've never actually met, but everyone knows her story. It was all over the papers a month ago, and then when her husband killed himself—"

"Daphne," Wolf said, a gentle warning in his tone.

"What?" she replied, clearly annoyed. "It's only my brother—I swear not to bring it up at the Everston ball next week."

Graham's mind was reeling. "Killed himself?"

Daphne nodded. "After he shot her. Well, not right after. A week or so went by, I suppose, and then they received a letter that he was going to toss himself into the river. Apparently, no one cared enough to stop him."

"How do you know all this?" Graham wondered, especially since he'd not heard a single detail of this story.

Daphne shrugged. "Word flies fast through the ton. I suppose a servant in their own household overheard something, and the next thing you know—"

"The Town gossips are feasting," Wolf finished.

"Oh, stop." Daphne waved him off with a flick of her hand. "He thinks I'm one of the Town gossips, but I'm not. Why, I've barely told a soul about any of this. It's not my fault someone told *me*."

Graham didn't much care who told whom—he could only think about Lady Beeston. No wonder there was such sadness behind her eyes. What kind of man would shoot his wife? Why, if she were his wife, he would never let harm come to her, let alone inflict it on her himself.

"Why did he shoot her?" he asked, for surely his sister knew that part of the story.

"Supposedly an accident on the field of honor. She tried to stop them and was caught in the crossfire."

"Then he was defending her honor?" At least there was that.

"Oh, no!" Daphne gave a somewhat maniacal laugh. "Her brother was defending her honor...*against* her husband."

"The duke?" Graham thought he must have heard wrong. Why would he have to defend her honor against her husband?

"No one knows exactly what sparked the duel, but it is common knowledge that Lord Beeston was...well, a beast. Fitting, isn't it?"

Graham was getting a headache. "I suppose." He felt rather sick to his stomach all of a sudden as the pieces began to fit together.

"Dinner is served," the butler announced from the doorway, but Graham had lost his appetite. For all the suffering he'd seen in his time as a doctor, it was alarming that this was disturbing him so. There was something about *her*. She seemed quite the most gentle woman he'd ever met, her demeanor so genuine, her eyes fathomless and soulful. One only need look at her to know the kind of person she was, and to think of a man—this Beeston—taking her for granted made Graham's blood boil. It was a good thing the man was dead already, for Graham would have a hard time not killing him.

"Graham, are you all right?" came Daphne's voice, snapping him from his thoughts.

"I think I'm not feeling well all of a sudden," he said, coming to his feet. "Would you be terribly upset if I didn't join you for dinner after all?"

Daphne took a large step away from him, whether consciously or not, he wasn't sure. "If you're ill, you ought to go home," she said. "Do you think you can make it? I could always have Evelyn make up a room for you."

Graham held up a hand. "No, no. I can make it home, I just...this headache came on rather quickly." As quickly as Daphne had told him the story of Lady Beeston.

He said his goodbyes and then made his way out to the street after gathering his things from the butler. Darkness was falling over the city as the lamplighters went about their work illuminating the sidewalks. Graham began his walk home, recounting his time that afternoon with Lady Beeston and then replaying his argument with the duke. She would never get better with Dr. Pritchard's methods. Laudanum would only weaken her until she wouldn't be able to so much as lift her head off the pillow, let alone try to walk again. Her muscles would begin to atrophy soon, and the poor woman would waste away to nothing.

Graham had always done his best to keep his emotions out of his practice. It was too difficult to become attached to a patient, only to have them die. Yet one afternoon in Lady Beeston's presence, and he had no choice. His heart was already in it. He wanted her to get better more than any other patient he'd ever cared for. He only had to figure out a way around the duke.

FIVE

There wasn't anything to get worked up over. Not a thing. He was only a doctor, just like Dr. Pritchard. He was going to tend to her and help her get better, and once she was better enough—for Dr. Pritchard had made it clear she would never be *completely* better—he would be on his way again. Never mind she'd spent half the night dreaming of him, or that the images and scenarios continued to swirl in her head in the light of day. He was still just a doctor.

Hannah craned her neck to see out the window. Not that she could see much from this far away, but if he were walking on the far side of the street, she might catch a glimpse of the top of his head.

Oh, it was no use. She slumped back to her pillow with a pout. He would be here when he was here—there was no point obsessing over where he might be now or when he might arrive.

She'd set her resolve to read some more, but just as she opened her book to the page she'd left off, the handle to her door jiggled. Her heart raced, and she sat there, stupefied, waiting to see who was on the other side.

"Good morning, Hannah."

Botheration, it was Mother. The Dowager Duchess of Somerset.

"Hello, Mother," Hannah replied, suddenly feeling like a little girl again, instead of a thirty-year-old woman. She hated that her mother had that power over her, yet she felt helpless to change it. "What brings you here today?"

"I live here, if you remember right," she said, her tone condescending and sharp, as always. She crossed the room, her black bombazine skirts swishing loudly in the silence, her hair refusing to move with the movement, thanks to her maid's tight hand and a thousand pins. "Are you feeling any better today?"

She asked that every day, as if Hannah might one morning leap from the bed and declare herself ready to reenter society. It was all about society for Mother. She lived and died by Debrett's, and expected everyone else to do the same. The society pages, more aptly referred to as the gossip columns, were as vital to her morning routine as tea and toast were. They were a source of life to her, which was why Hannah and her mother had never really understood one another.

Of course, Mother had come 'round after the shooting, defending her against Beeston—something she'd never done before. Not in the ten long, lonely years that Hannah had suffered as his wife. But she supposed her mother's change of heart—however short lived—was something to celebrate.

"A bit," Hannah finally answered. "But when the laudanum wears off again..."

"You'll just take more," Mother finished.

Hannah sighed. "But I don't like to take it. It makes me sleepy."

"Rest is what you need. That's why Dr. Pritchard prescribed the stuff to you."

And yet Dr. Alcott seemed to disagree with him on that point. "I think I'm tired of resting," she blurted out.

The dowager turned sharply to look at her. "Rest is vital for your recovery."

Hannah knew she was treading on shaky ground, picking an argument with her mother, but she couldn't help it. She was bored. "Is it? It's been nearly two months and my condition is hardly changed."

"Well, it hasn't worsened." Her mother was getting agitated, if her flaring nostrils were any indication. "Now, see here, you will do exactly as the doctor dictates, do you understand?"

HOW TO CARE FOR A LADY

Hannah allowed herself a small smile. Of course she would. But clearly, Mother didn't know she was no longer under the care of Dr. Pritchard.

"I think that's a very wise idea," came a masculine voice from the doorway.

"Who are you?" Mother asked, her voice as stern and biting as ever as she looked Dr. Alcott up and down with a shrewd eye. Clearly, she was scandalized that a handsome man was in Hannah's bedchamber.

Hannah couldn't stop her heart from fluttering or her toes from tingling at the sight of him, for he was indeed very handsome. She might never get over how tall he seemed, even in her rather large bedchamber. And the way the light streamed in through the windows, catching his sandy hair just so, made the strands of gold shimmer brightly. But it was the way he looked at her that truly made it hard to catch her breath. Did he look at all his patients that way?

"Mother," she finally managed, "this is Dr. Alcott. He has taken over for Dr. Pritchard. Dr. Alcott, may I introduce you to the Dowager Duchess of Somerset, who is, coincidentally, my mother."

~*~

One could immediately see why Hannah was as meek and quiet as she was—someone else had clearly been speaking on her behalf her entire life. The dowager duchess was a formidable woman with a sharp tongue, and Graham had deduced that in a mere thirty seconds. If he thought the duke had been intimidating, his mother was one hundred times more so.

He bowed to the woman, nonetheless. "An honor, Your Grace," he said, and then righted himself once again.

"Where is Dr. Pritchard?"

Apparently, she wasn't one for pleasantries.

"He is gone, Mother," the baroness answered before Graham even had a chance to open his mouth. "The Countess of Kilworth has requested his presence during her confinement, and he cannot care for both of us, what with her being in the country—"

"This is an outrage!" The dowager's skin had turned to an unnatural shade of purple, and she nearly shook with rage. "He valued a *countess* over *you*?"

"In truth, I am only a baron's widow."

"Yes, but your brother is a duke," Her Grace bit back, "and *he* is the one paying for your care."

"Perhaps I could find it in myself to be as overset about this as you are if I didn't have a great deal of confidence in his replacement." She smiled up at Graham, and it warmed him all over. "As it stands, I'm very happy with Dr. Alcott."

Graham smiled back, completely locked in her gaze. "Thank you," he said with a slight bow of his head.

The dowager stared at him, her lips drawn together in a straight line, her nostrils flaring with each breath. "What credentials have you?" she demanded.

"He comes on recommendation from Dr. Pritchard, Mother. What more do you need?"

Graham appreciated her defense, but he didn't want the dowager to think he couldn't fight his own battles. "Quite a few, actually," he said. "My father was a doctor, and I grew up watching and learning from him. After his death, I became the local doctor in our town, and eventually was honored with an apprenticeship here in London, with Dr. Pritchard. I've been working with him for six years now, while also attending lectures and symposiums on medical advancements. Does that satisfy Your Grace?"

Perhaps he should have left off that last bit—it did come across as rather goading. But he couldn't help himself. The woman was intolerable, and he'd only been in her presence a mere few minutes.

She narrowed her beady eyes on him and straightened her spine. Graham didn't dare look at Lady Beeston, for she was likely trying to keep a straight face. It wouldn't be terribly professional to burst into laughter just then.

"I will sit here while you see to my daughter today," the dowager finally said, slipping onto the tufted window seat.

Graham finally turned to Lady Beeston. "Is that all right with you?" he asked.

She nodded, though a bit reluctantly, it seemed. "I'm certain I don't have another choice." Then she sent a pointed look to her mother.

After an awkward moment of silence, Graham sprang into action, trying to put all this nonsense behind him. "Well, then. Let us begin." He moved across the room and set his large, black bag down on the night table, knocking over the bottle of what he assumed was laudanum at the same time.

Lady Beeston gasped and reached for the vial as if she were a rabid dog. Once she had it in her grasp, she slowly looked up until she met Graham's eyes, before quickly looking away again. Damn.

"Sorry," she muttered. "I just didn't want it to drip to the rug."

Right. "Thankfully the lid was on tightly. No harm done."

She cleared her throat. "No harm done," she repeated. "So, what are you going to force me to do today?"

"First," he said, plucking the bottle from her hands again and placing it further away, atop the dresser. Her eyes followed it carefully. Was she worried about how she would get to it in his absence? "First, we will ring to have a bath drawn."

"A bath?" the dowager called from her spot by the window. "Is that safe?"

"I have already been through this with Dr. Alcott, Mother." She turned up her lovely brown eyes at him. "He assures me it is perfectly safe."

"I'm going to dress the wound," he went on to explain, breaking the startling eye contact she'd initiated and addressing the dowager. "I shall attempt to keep it as dry as possible."

"You don't mean to say that *you're* going to bathe her?" the dowager balked.

Graham looked back to Lady Beeston, who's face was flushed a bright pink. She was now trying desperately to avoid eye contact.

"No," Graham said, laughing just a bit in spite of the fact the idea of bathing her was quite arousing. Damn. He must keep himself in check. She was a patient. Nothing more. Perhaps he needed a visit to a local madam to ease his ardor. It wouldn't do to go springing up every time he was in her presence. "No, of course not," he went on. "Once the wound is properly dressed, I will step out of the room while your maid bathes you. When you're finished, I will return to apply a poultice. Then I will let you rest."

"No walk today?"

Oh, how he wanted to walk with her. To have his arm around her waist again and feel her slight body pressed into his side. "Not today. The bath will be taxing enough."

The dowager shook her head as she made her way to the bell pull in the corner of the room. She tugged on one of the bells, and then tsked. "I don't know how I feel about this, Dr. Alcott, but I will defer to your expertise...for now."

"Thank you, Your Grace. Your confidence means the world."

And truly, it did. Getting past the duke was one thing; pleasing the dowager was a feat of a whole different nature. To get her approval—even if temporary—felt like a victory.

"May I?" he asked Lady Beeston as the dowager returned to her spot by the window.

The baroness nodded, though her lashes fluttered and she looked away from him. Clearly, she found this part uncomfortable, and Graham did too, for the first time in his career. He'd cared for many a pretty lady, but none like her. Lady Beeston, in spite of the fact she hadn't had a bath in far too long, had captivated him. It was easy to see she was a beautiful woman, even with matted hair and a sallow complexion. He could see past that, right to her heart.

"How does it feel today?" he asked as he pulled yesterday's bandage from her leg with as gentle a hand as he could manage.

"Sore, but perhaps not as bad as before."

"Have you taken any laudanum today?"

There was a pause. Her throat worked as she swallowed loudly. "Yes," she finally answered, and there was shame in her tone.

She ought not to feel ashamed. Laudanum was the cure-all in their world. But he wanted to show her a better way—a different way. He'd seen what the stuff could do to people over time, the way it held them in its grasp and wouldn't let go. Oftentimes, the effects of the medicine turned out to be worse than the ailment in the first place. With a poultice of ancient herbs and oils, perhaps they could simply treat the wound and not her entire person.

The maid arrived while Graham tended to the wound, and at the dowager's instruction began the process of preparing Lady Beeston's bath. When it was time for him to make his exit, Graham found it hard to leave—almost as if his feet were refusing to move.

"Dr. Alcott," the dowager said sharply as he stood lamely at Lady Beeston's bedside.

"My apologies," he said, coming to. "I will wait downstairs until you are ready for me."

Unable to look her in the eyes, Graham left the room, stopping to catch his breath once outside the door. His breath and his heart, God help him.

SIX

Hannah sat in the small wooden chair while a maid dumped the last bucket of warm water into the large copper tub. She was a bit nervous, truth be known, which was preposterous. It wasn't as if she'd never taken a bath before. But it had been a long time, and part of her worried that Dr. Alcott was being too aggressive with his treatments.

She gulped down her apprehension. Something had to change. Something had to give—either she would die or get better. But she couldn't stay in that bed wasting away the rest of her life.

"Are you ready, my lady?" her maid, Alice, asked. She'd not had much use for her over the last couple months. Her brother had a staff of thirty, and seeing as Hannah hadn't been out of bed, well, Alice had been scarce.

Hannah stared at the tub for a long moment and then finally nodded. Alice took her by the elbow, slowly and gently guiding her to the tub. Hannah swung her good leg over the edge and into the water. It was warm, but not *too* warm, on Dr. Alcott's instructions. Poor Alice was forced to support the bulk of her weight while helping to lift her wounded leg over the edge. In truth, they could have used an extra pair of hands to help her in, but obviously, Dr. Alcott couldn't be one of them, and Mother had taken herself off to do her correspondence. But it was too late to call for an extra maid, so they had to make do, carefully, slowly, until at last Hannah was sinking her body into the warm cocoon of water.

"Oh, Alice," she sighed. "How I have missed this!"

"Unfortunately, I can't let you linger, my lady."

"Yes, I know," Hannah replied. Dr. Alcott had made it clear that she not luxuriate in the water too long, lest the bandage be breached by the water. She was to get in, wash, and get out. "Go on."

Alice set to washing her, starting at her hair and face, then moving on to the rest of her body, finishing with her feet. The smell of rose oil and lye wafted about her, sending shockwaves of joy and relief through her body. How wonderful it felt to finally be washing off the dregs of the last many weeks. With every stroke of Alice's washcloth, Hannah felt renewed.

"If you can stand, my lady, I've another clean bucket of water to do the final rinse."

Whatever it took, Hannah would find a way to stand long enough to be rinsed. The water in the tub was gray by the end—if she wasn't going to rinse it off, she might as well not have taken a bath at all. "I will try, but you must help me get there."

Hannah placed her hands on the edge on the tub, using it as a cantilever to pull herself up, while Alice pushed from behind. It was all rather humiliating, being completely helpless and relying on everyone else to push or pull or hold her weight. She silently prayed that Dr. Alcott knew what he was saying when he purported that she would walk again.

She winced as she came to her feet, the effort sending waves of pain to her wound. Stars danced before her eyes, and she worried, momentarily, that she might fall back down into the filthy water.

"You're shaking, my lady," Alice said, alarm lacing her tone.

Hannah took a deep breath and blew it out slowly. "I'll be all right," she promised, not wanting to alarm her maid. "Let us rinse me and get me back to bed as soon as possible."

She hunched over, holding on to the edge of the tub, but when the deluge of water came over her, she lost her balance, and went tumbling back into the tub with a scream.

~*~

Graham had been unable to keep still in the parlor after giving explicit orders to Cook for his poultice, so he'd decided to come back upstairs and simply pace the corridor until he was called back in. But the scream he'd just heard coming from her chambers was good enough.

He burst through the door and followed the sounds of commotion to her ladyship's dressing room, where they'd set up the bath.

The little maid was leaning over the copper tub, speaking calmly to her mistress, while Hannah shook and struggled to get out of her grasp. Damn it all. She'd gone into some kind of shock.

"What happened?" he demanded, coming to the other side of the tub.

"Dr. Alcott!" The maid was clearly scandalized at his presence, but this was no time for propriety.

"Get me a towel."

She did as she was told, and then held the towel open, awaiting further instruction. Graham lifted Hannah easily from the tub and held her trembling body against him, no matter she was dripping wet and clothed only in a thin, wet bathing gown. Surely her family would be horrified, but he was a doctor, for God's sake. A fact of which he had to keep reminding himself when in the presence of Lady Beeston.

He sat on the wooden chair nearby, with her still in his arms. "Bring me the towel."

The maid crossed the room and handed over the large, white cloth that had been heated for Lady Beeston's comfort. He wrapped it around her shoulders, and her body immediately relaxed against his. Thank God.

Her eyes, which had been wild and unfocused, fluttered closed as she sucked in deep breaths. Graham resisted the urge to rock her or kiss her forehead—that would surely be crossing some kind of line. Instead, he held her firmly and watched her face, waiting for her to come to.

"What in the world is going on in here?" came the sharp tones of the dowager duchess.

Graham took a steadying breath—wasn't it enough he'd failed Lady Beeston? And now he had to suffer criticism from her shrew of a mother.

"She fell, Your Grace," he said, steeling himself for her blows.

"This is *your* fault," she said.

And just as Graham was about to open his mouth to both apologize and defend himself, the little maid whimpered and muttered an apology of her own. Graham looked up to find the dowager's beady gaze fixed on the young girl. The poor thing.

"It most certainly is not," Graham said, trying to keep calm in spite of the outrage he felt on the girl's behalf. "She was only trying to do her job, and admittedly, that job required more than one small maid. I should have insisted there be another set of hands."

The dowager, thankfully, looked properly chastised, even if she did try to hide it behind a steely façade. "Well, then…you live another day, Alice."

"Alice, would you be so kind as to retrieve the poultice from the kitchen? It should be ready by now."

The little maid sniffed and nodded her head eagerly before running from the room. Graham couldn't help but feel for the girl—or anyone who was forced to come into contact with this woman, really. She was the very antithesis of pleasant. However, she was all Graham had at the moment.

"We need to get her into dry clothing."

The dowager stared down her long nose at him. "Then you shouldn't have sent Alice away."

"You and I can more easily handle the task, I think. And besides, I think she's been through enough."

"Oh, has she?" Her Grace bit back. "I rather think Alice failed in her duties today—it is my daughter who has been through a rough time."

"I didn't say otherwise. It goes without saying that Lady Beeston is suffering greatly. But she's resting peacefully now, whereas the maid is quite shaken up from—as you put it —*failing* her mistress."

"If you think you're going to participate in undressing my daughter, you are sorely mistaken."

"Then I shall leave her in your capable hands, madam."

The woman sucked in a sharp breath. "I will have you removed from this house post haste, Dr. Alcott. I will not tolerate such disrespect from someone in your position."

Damn. He didn't want to get himself dismissed. Lady Beeston needed him, and she was his primary concern. He could make nice with this shrew if it meant keeping his post.

"I'm sorry," he choked out. The words tasted like dust on his tongue. "I mean no disrespect. Perhaps you could ring for more help, then? Even when Alice does return, she is not capable of doing this alone—not when Lady Beeston is fast asleep and unable to assist."

This seemed to douse the flames a bit, and the dowager did as he suggested, making her way through the next chamber and ringing the bell pull. Within minutes, they'd gathered a team of maids, including Alice, who had returned with the poultice. Graham waited outside the room while they changed her, and when they were done, and all but the dowager had left, he reentered the room, ready to apply the poultice.

But when he saw her, his feet came to a halt on the thin rug beneath his feet. If he'd thought her beautiful before, she was a thousand times more so now. They'd left her hair unbound, and the long locks of slightly damp curls framed her face and tumbled over her shoulders. They were the color of coffee, dark and rich and shiny. There was color in her cheeks now, presumably from the warmth of her bath. And her eyes fluttered, as if she were deep inside a dream. To think of all this woman had been through broke his heart, for she deserved only the most wonderful things that the world had to offer.

"Much better, isn't it?" the dowager asked, her voice actually low and relaxed for a change.

"She will certainly feel better," he replied, not wanting to admit to finding her breathtakingly beautiful. "I am hoping this poultice," he continued, moving to where the maid had left the concoction on the bureau, "will make her feel even better still."

"What is in this poultice of yours?"

"Oils," he said simply.

"Oils?"

"Derived from plants and flowers. They have been using them for centuries in the East."

"No doubt you learned of them in one of your symposiums."

Actually, he'd learned it from what some might refer to as a witch doctor, but there was no need to share that bit of information. "One can learn a great deal from these lectures and symposiums," he replied. It wasn't a lie, but it wasn't the whole truth.

The dowager walked to the other side of the bed as Graham pulled back the covers to reveal Lady Beeston's leg. They'd dressed her in a fresh nightgown, made of soft, white cotton. She looked like an angel lying there, and it was all Graham could do to keep himself from crawling into the bed and holding her against him until she forgot every nasty word that had been said to her, every horrific act committed against her. But he couldn't ever do that. It would be in his best interest to assume a more professional view of his patient.

"Will it hurt her?"

It seemed odd that the woman cared whether the poultice would hurt or not, but he answered her just the same. "Perhaps, a bit. Some of the oils can be a bit...hot, for lack of a better term. But hopefully she is sleeping deeply enough that she won't notice."

With that hope in mind, he lifted the baroness's gown to reveal her wound, unbound it, and then pressed a cloth laden with the concoction against her leg.

SEVEN

Stinging pain cut through the hazy blackness of sleep, jarring Hannah awake. What the devil was happening to her?

"You're all right," came a gentle voice. A voice that calmed her and excited her all at once.

Her eyes flew open, taking in the light, her mother, and finally, Dr. Alcott. "It hurts," she cried, squeezing her eyes shut again against the pain.

"Just breathe," he said. "It will subside, I swear to you."

She did as she was told, though it wasn't easy. She wanted to writhe and scream, but she tried to focus on her breath, in and out, in and out...

It didn't take long, but he'd been right. The pain began to subside, little by little, until it left only a tingling sensation in her wound.

"Can I persuade you into giving me my laudanum?" she asked, and his brow immediately knitted into a frown.

He perched himself on the edge of the bed, the concern in his hazel eyes unsettling her. "Lady Beeston, may I ask how much laudanum you've been taking in a day?"

Hannah swallowed over the lump in her throat. The truth was, she'd been taking quite a bit more than Dr. Pritchard had prescribed, but Dr. Alcott didn't need to know that, did he? "One teaspoon every three hours, just as Dr. Pritchard prescribed."

Dr. Alcott nodded, clearly deep in thought. "Let us try moving that to every four hours, shall we?"

The thought alone made Hannah twitch, especially since she'd been taking *two* teaspoons every three hours. But if his poultice worked, perhaps she could stretch the time and reduce the dose. "We can certainly try it," she said, trying to sound more confident than she felt.

Finally, that yielded a smile from the doctor. She very much liked when he smiled.

"Good. I think it is time I take my leave. You need your rest after the ordeal you've had."

Hannah tried to think back, but the last thing she remembered was being in the bathtub. Goodness, how had she gotten here? Heat infused her cheeks instantaneously as she considered the possibility that Dr. Alcott could have been the one to bring her to the bed and—

"What happened?" she asked, directing the question to her mother, for she couldn't possibly make eye contact with Dr. Alcott right now.

"You fell," Mother replied, matter-of-factly. "Dr. Alcott had to rescue you."

"He did?" the words came out as barely a whisper. Heavens, why did she feel so self-conscious? He was a *doctor*. Surely he'd seen a woman in a bathing gown. Oh, Lord! Her stomach churned at the thought of the thin, white fabric clinging to her otherwise naked body. Had he been the one to peel it off her and replace it with this nightgown? This never would have happened with Dr. Pritchard, for she never would have left the bed in the first place.

"I did," Dr. Alcott confirmed as he packed his things back into his black bag. "But Alice and some of the other maids got you into dry clothes."

Thank heavens for that.

"I suppose I should thank you," she said, still avoiding eye contact with him.

But then she could feel his eyes boring into her—he was waiting for her to look at him. When she did, there was such kindness in his face, in his eyes, it nearly took her breath away.

"I will always do whatever I must to ensure your health and safety," he said, his voice low and genuine.

Hannah swallowed again and gave him a little nod before Mother broke the spell.

"I will see you out, Dr. Alcott."

He nodded and smiled at Hannah. "Until tomorrow." Then he followed Mother to the hallway.

Just as they were about to close the door behind them, Hannah realized her bottle of laudanum was still far away, upon the bureau. Panic seized her and she called out before she could stop herself.

"Wait!"

The door swung open again and Dr. Alcott blinked at her, waiting, as she'd requested.

"The, um...the laudanum," she said sheepishly, feeling ashamed and desperate at the same time. "You left it over there."

Dr. Alcott looked toward the bureau, and for a long moment, Hannah wondered if he was going to leave it there, out of her reach. But finally, he said, "Indeed, I did," and then moved across the room to retrieve the bottle.

He brought it to her bedside and held it in his hands. "I beg of you to give the poultice a chance," he said, his tone grave, his hazel eyes pleading.

Hannah nodded. "You have my word."

He stared at her for another long moment and then finally placed the bottle on the nightstand. Relief washed through Hannah as he walked away and closed the door behind him. As soon as he was gone, and in spite of her promise, she reached for the bottle.

~*~

Graham wasn't at all surprised that the duke met them in the foyer downstairs. He was waiting by the door, his arms folded over his broad chest, his dark curls practically shaking with fury. Thank God the dowager stood by him, though he never thought *she* would be the one he'd take comfort in.

"What the devil are you doing to my sister?" the duke demanded as Graham and the dowager reached the last step.

"Now, Evan, you needn't get so worked up over it," Her Grace said before Graham had a chance to even open his mouth. "Hannah is fine and resting peacefully now."

"Stay out of this, Mother." The duke put a hand up to his mother and focused his attention on Graham. But Graham still would not get to say his piece.

"How *dare* you dismiss me like that?" The older woman stepped in front of Graham to force her son to look at her. "She is my daughter. Do you think I would allow harm to come to her?"

It was clear the duke was seriously considering his words in that moment, and Graham had a feeling it had to do with a long history of the dowager turning the other way. Somerset would be wise not to point that out, if it was, in fact, the case, but Graham still held his breath, lest it come to blows.

"Need I remind you this is *my* house, Mother?" the duke bit back.

"Then throw me out!"

"What is going on out here?"

A young woman with flaxen hair appeared from the drawing room, her eyes wide with curiosity.

"Everything is fine, darling," the duke said. "We're just trying to sort out this whole debacle."

"You must be Dr. Alcott," the woman—presumably the Duchess of Somerset—said, coming into the foyer and reaching out a hand to him.

Graham took it and bowed to her. "At your service, Your Grace."

"I've heard so much about you, Doctor."

"Not all bad, I hope," he said, daring a glance at the still-fuming duke.

"Not from Hannah. She seems quite fond of you."

Something about that warmed his heart, though it shouldn't have. It was surely on a professional level that she thought fondly of him.

"That is nice to hear," he replied.

"Fond or not, this man has endangered my sister, and I won't stand for it," the duke snarled. "You promised me no harm would come to her."

"And no harm *has* come to her," the dowager quipped. "She merely slipped—it could happen to anyone."

"But it happened to *her.*"

"Perhaps the two of you should go and argue in private," the young duchess suggested, causing both the affronted parties to clamp their lips together. Quite impressive, if you asked Graham. She seemed to lack any fear of the two of them, and to be truthful, they were both quite fearsome characters. "Now," she said, turning back to Graham. "As long as Hannah is happy with you as her doctor, then you shall remain her doctor."

"But—"

She held up a hand to silence her husband. "Hannah is thirty years old, Evan. For heaven's sake, let the woman make her own choices. Heaven knows it's been far too long since she's been allowed to do so."

The more Graham learned about her past, the more curious he became. "Thank you, Your Grace," he said, and then turned to the duke. "And please know, I do not take any of this lightly. No one was as shaken as I was by today's events. Your sister's health and safety are of the utmost importance to me."

"Then I shan't expect another episode such as this one," the duke bit back. He wasn't happy, that much was clear, but he wasn't letting him go. He didn't seem to have much of a choice in the matter.

"I will endeavor to prevent one ever again."

The duchess called for the butler then, and once he'd donned his hat and cane, Graham left the house, grateful to be free of the duke and his mother, and ever more so that he'd get to see Lady Beeston on the morrow.

EIGHT

"Well, well, well, we thought you'd never awaken."

Hannah blinked as she tried to register whose voice was speaking to her. Goodness, her body felt heavy, and her eyelids, too, for that matter. Was she under water? For that's what it felt like. Like she was drowning.

"Water?" came the voice again, and Hannah finally opened her eyes enough to see the pale blonde head of her sister-in-law.

"Grace?" she mumbled, but it felt as if there was a ball of cotton in her mouth.

"Yes, dear, it's me. Have some water." Hannah tried to sit up, but her body wouldn't allow it, so Grace put an arm around her neck and lifted her head to the glass. "There you are."

The cool water made its way down her throat, taking that fuzzy feeling with it.

"Better?" Grace asked.

Hannah nodded. "Much. What time is it?"

"Late." Grace placed the water glass on the side table and then perched on the edge of the bed. "Dr. Alcott will be here soon. Would you like something to eat?"

"He's probably going to make me walk today, so I ought to have something in my stomach."

"I'll ring for your meal, then."

Grace went about the room, calling for and speaking to the maid, then tidying up, even though there was nothing to tidy. She just kept picking things up and putting them back exactly where they'd been before. After several minutes of this, Hannah had had enough.

"Grace?" she said, halting her sister-in-law's practices.

Grace stared at her with those wide, emerald eyes. "Yes?"

"Is something the matter?"

"Ehm…" she looked away and fiddled with a perfume bottle on the vanity. "Not *wrong,* really. Just…"

"Come now, Grace," Hannah pleaded. "Whatever it is, you can tell me. I promise your secret is safe with me."

"Well, that is just the thing." Grace looked up and swallowed. "It isn't a secret. As a matter of fact, you shall be the last to know."

Hannah was starting to get irritated. What on earth was the matter with her sister-in-law? "Grace, I swear if you don't tell me soon, I shall lunge from this bed and force you to tell me."

Of course, they both knew that wasn't true, but still, she had a point to get across.

"All right, fine." Grace took a deep breath, her chest puffing up as her head lolled back to look at the ceiling. "The thing is…that is to say…"

"Grace!"

"I'm expecting!"

The world stood still. Everything fell silent. The only sound the whooshing of Hannah's own breath in her ears. Her heart constricted, and tears filled her eyes.

"Oh, Lud! I knew I shouldn't have told you." Grace rushed to her side, nestling on the edge of the bed and taking her hand. "I'm so sorry."

"Don't you dare be sorry," Hannah chastised her, while trying to swallow down the lump in her throat. "Just because I can't have children doesn't mean *you* shouldn't, for heaven's sake."

"The last thing I wanted to do was upset you, but it was going to come out sooner or later, and I didn't want you to hear it from someone else."

"And I wouldn't have *wanted* to hear it from someone else. I am so very happy for you, my dear Grace."

"Truly?" Grace asked, her green eyes desperate for approval.

"Truly."

And then Grace threw herself onto Hannah. Hannah hugged her back with a squeeze.

"Goodness, you can't know how nervous I was to tell you," her sister-in-law said as she sat up straight again. "Or how relieved I am to have done so."

"Well, I'm sure it was a great burden, trying to keep it from me."

They chatted on for a few minutes, and Hannah did her best to pretend she was all right. But in truth, she felt as if she were dying inside. Her heart ached, and her stomach churned. Was it possible to be so very distraught for herself, while also being thrilled for her brother and Grace? It seemed quite impossible, and yet, those two paradoxical emotions warred within her.

Hannah's lunch tray arrived, but she'd lost her appetite completely. Instead of saying so to Grace, she simply sent her sister-in-law on an errand for her.

"Peonies!" she said, to which Grace blinked at her with great confusion on her brow. "I think they would brighten up the room, don't you?"

"I suppose so. You don't have any flowers, do you?"

Hannah shook her head, even though the statement was quite rhetorical, for one could plainly see there were no flowers in the room. "Perhaps you would be so kind as to go and get some?"

"Me?"

It was odd, sending her and not a servant, but Hannah wanted to be alone without telling her why. "You have such lovely taste. Please."

That seemed to fluff her sense of pride. She smiled broadly. "All right, if you insist. I shall bring them back soon, I promise."

"Don't rush on my account," Hannah replied with a forced smile.

Grace bounced out of the room and not a moment too soon. Hannah couldn't hold back anymore. Ten years. Ten years she'd lain with that vile man, praying for a child, waiting, month after month in hopeful expectation, only to be let down over and over again. And then to know that Grace, who had been married to Evan less than a few months, was already with child... It was selfish and horrible of her to think this way, but she couldn't help it. She wanted it to be her. She wanted to know what it was like to carry a baby in her belly. To know the joys of motherhood. And even the hardships! She wanted it all. But now here she was, a wounded widow, barren, completely pathetic.

The sobs came harder, robbing her of her breath. As she attempted to get herself under control, wiping her eyes and breathing as deeply as her lungs would allow, the bottle of laudanum caught her eye. She'd taken twice her dosage last night, which probably accounted for how late she'd slept today and how groggy she felt, but at least she had slept, hadn't she? At least she hadn't been forced to lie awake, thinking of all the ways her life had gone wrong. All the wrong decisions she'd made, the people she'd trusted and ought not to have. It took away the ache, and that was more important to her than anything just then.

Somehow that little bottle gave her new hope. Her sobs subsided, and she wiped her eyes before she reached determinedly for the bottle and spoon, uncorked the bottle, and began to pour the syrup onto the spoon. She swallowed down the first spoonful and then poised to pour once again.

"I do hope you're not planning to take more than that, my lady."

The unexpected presence in her room startled her into dropping the bottle. Panic settled in as she looked over the edge of the bed and saw the syrup spilling onto the rug. She looked to Dr. Alcott, expecting to see him rushing to her aid, but he only stood there, staring at her, complete and utter disappointment on his features.

"Dr. Alcott," she breathed, feeling like a child who'd been caught stealing sweetmeats from the confectioner's. "I didn't hear you come in."

"No," he replied. "I don't suppose you did."

She looked down at the rug again, now stained with almost the entire contents of the bottle, then back to Dr. Alcott. "The bottle," she said lamely, as if he didn't already know it was there.

"I will ring for a maid to pick it up."

"But there may be time to save the rest," she cried, unable to control the panic she felt rising in her breast. "Won't you pick it up?"

He looked to the bottle, and then to her. "No, I will not." He crossed the room until he was at her bedside. "You sent your sister-in-law out for flowers?"

Blast it all. Hannah looked away, feeling foolish. "I thought they might brighten up the room."

She dared a glance at him. He was staring at her, his features softening just a bit. She wondered what he was thinking—to be honest, the way he stared at her made her feel just the slightest bit of longing. Part of her wanted to reach out and pull him against her, feel his arms around her, tell him she was sorry for lying. But of course she didn't. That wouldn't be terribly proper of her. And besides, he was her doctor. It was his job to be kind and caring toward her, wasn't it? Dr. Pritchard had always been kind, but then she'd thought of him more as a father figure than, well...

"Goodness, it's warm in here, isn't it?" she said, pulling at the collar of her nightgown.

"It's actually quite lovely out today. What would you think about venturing to the garden?"

He might as well have suggested they venture to the moon! "I couldn't possibly, Dr. Alcott. Why, I barely made it to the staircase the other day, and yesterday...well, I'm not feeling terribly confident right now."

"But how are you feeling otherwise? Your leg, I mean?"

"My leg? Oh, well, I suppose it's a little better."

"Then why were you going to take another spoonful of laudanum?"

This last was asked with such grave seriousness that Hannah was hardly able to respond. For a long moment, she just sat there, staring at him, wondering what to tell him. The truth was always an option, she supposed. But she'd spent the last ten years appearing weak and meek to a man who gladly took advantage of her as a result. She wasn't quite ready to let her guard down with this one, even if he was her doctor. But then, he'd caught her out, hadn't he? Perhaps she could share only the most recent of disturbing events.

She cleared her throat and looked away. The way he stared at her made it very hard to look at him. If she looked too long, she would fa—

She stopped that thought in its tracks. Ludicrous. It was just that he was nice to her and not a relation. That was all.

"My sister-in-law," she finally managed. "She delivered some news to me just a bit ago."

"Bad news, I assume?"

"Actually," Hannah gave an ironic little laugh, "quite good news! She is with child. Isn't that just wonderful?"

She wasn't fooling anyone, least of all *him*. He took her hand, which was shaking, much to her embarrassment. He patted it a few times and then looked her directly in the eye, nearly spearing her with his golden gaze. "It is high time you start living your life, my lady," he said, and it seemed his words held something unspoken.

"Is that not what I have been doing?" Hannah replied, feigning confusion, even though she knew his words were not literal in the least.

"I don't know your entire story, Lady Beeston, but I think I know enough. And I think we need to get you walking again." He raised his slender eyebrows. "Dancing again?"

"I haven't danced in years, Doctor," she laughed. "My husband wasn't the sort."

"How unfortunate. I imagine you are quite graceful on the dance floor."

"I was," she corrected. "But I doubt I will be again. Out of practice and with a bullet hole in my leg—I hardly think those make for graceful dancing."

"I admit, I'm not the most graceful myself..." There he was again, looking at her like *that*. "Perhaps one day I will persuade you to stand up with me."

"Even if I went out in society again, it—"

She broke off, realizing what she was about to say— that *he* would never be invited to any type of ball or party that *she* would. Although, now she thought about it, there was a great deal of scandal around her now. Who knew what the gossips were saying about her? It was quite possible she'd not be welcomed into society ever again.

"I'm sorry," she said, sobering.

"Don't be. I'm used to being left behind, what with my sister being a viscountess and all."

"Oh?" Hannah was certain she'd not heard about his sister before. Or had she? Maybe he'd said something about her marrying a Londoner. He'd omitted the part about the Londoner being a peer of the realm.

"Viscountess Wolverly," he clarified. "Her husband goes by Wolf."

"Oh, my," Hannah breathed. She'd had no idea. "Why, I've attended quite a few functions at their home in the past. I didn't realize Lady Wolverly had a doctor for a brother."

"Few people do. I prefer a quieter life. Part of me wishes I could return to Ravenglass."

"It's nice there?"

Dr. Alcott nodded. "Lovely. Especially in the autumn, when the leaves turn red and orange, and the weather turns cool. Before the snow, of course. Makes it rather difficult to make house calls when the town is buried in snow."

"I can imagine."

"Now," he said, standing to his full, impressive height. "How about that walk?"

NINE

Graham wasn't certain how he accomplished it, but he finally got the widow to agree to a walk to the garden. She walked the length of the corridor with some improvement over their walk the other day, and then he carried her down the stairs to the main floor. Servants stared in shock before offering smiles and curtsies for the baroness, and the attention seemed to be quite encouraging to her. Even when no one was watching, she was still smiling. It made Graham quite happy to see.

When they reached the doors to the outside, she paused, preventing him from moving forward. "What is it?" he asked.

Her eyes were fixed on the gardens. "I haven't been outside for so long—I just want to savor the moment."

Graham couldn't help but chuckle a bit at that. "I can't blame you. I think I would quite go out of my mind were I to be forced inside for more than a few days, let alone nearly two months."

There was silence as she stared a moment longer, and then, "I'm ready."

They hobbled through the door and out onto the veranda. It was warm, but there was a gentle breeze that brought the smell of lilacs with it. Graham could feel Lady Beeston's slight body heaving deep breaths, taking in the sights and the smells all at once.

"How do you feel?" he asked.

"Like I'm being reborn," she replied. "Like I'm learning to breathe for the first time."

"You're glad you came, then?"

Finally, she turned her chocolate brown eyes up to look at him. She was so beautiful with her hair tumbling over her shoulders, a few errant strands tossing about in the breeze. He ought not to think of her this way, but he couldn't help himself.

"I think you might never get me back inside," she laughed.

"Come," he said, guiding her toward the divan near the end of the verandah. "You can sit here and enjoy the breeze."

"You won't stay?" she asked, blinking at him with hopefulness in her eyes.

I would never leave if I didn't have to. "I need to instruct Cook to prepare your poultice. Would you like me to order a repast while I'm at it?"

"Something sweet," she said with a smile. "And some tea, perhaps?"

"I won't be long."

Graham reluctantly left her resting alone on the divan and hurried inside to find Cook. Unfortunately, he found someone else first.

"Dr. Alcott," the duke said, as Graham passed the open door of the man's study.

There was nothing for it. "Afternoon, Your Grace," he replied with a bow.

"How is my sister?" he asked, without preamble.

"Progressing," Graham replied.

"Already? And even after her setback in the bath?"

"Sometimes a setback can catapult us to the next milestone. You may see her yourself, if you like. She is on the verandah, waiting for me to call for tea."

The duke stared at him, his eyebrows raised, his head cocked in such a manner that indicated he wasn't pleased at this news. "I'm confused," he said, his tone more than just a little biting. "Are you here as a *doctor* or as a *suitor*?"

The question caused heat to rush to Graham's face. The thought of being more than just her doctor had crossed his mind more times than it ought to have. "Getting her fresh air and a bit of exercise for the leg is part of the treatment," he said, his voice steadier than he'd expected it to be. "The tea is for her, not for me."

"Hm." The duke nodded and drummed his fingers on his desk. "Carry on, then. I do think I shall go have a visit with my sister."

"I'm certain she will enjoy that, Your Grace."

Graham gratefully bowed out of the room, desperate to have a moment alone to calm his breath and his racing heart. He took his time on his way to the kitchen, knowing the duke was going to see his sister, and then he meandered his way back to the verandah once he'd delivered his instructions.

Somerset sat on a chair beside the divan—the chair Graham had planned to sit in himself. But it wasn't as if he could order the duke to find another seat. That would surely raise suspicions, in addition to being completely out of line.

They spoke in hushed tones, so Graham had no idea what they were talking about, but as soon as Lady Beeston spotted him, she smiled broadly, and said, "Dr. Alcott! Did Cook have something sweet for me?"

"Indeed, she did," he said. "It will be here soon, she promises."

"Hannah was just telling me about your sister, the viscountess," the duke said. "I didn't realize you had such relations."

"I don't usually go about announcing it." Graham took a seat on the other side of the small table from Somerset. "But yes, Lady Wolverly is indeed my sister."

The duke glanced at his sister. "You know Grace is going to want to have them for dinner."

Lady Beeston looked to Graham. "Perhaps when my doctor says I am able enough to attend a meal at the table?"

"It shouldn't be long," he replied. "Why, you look quite well today, even."

"I still think you should take things slowly." The duke furrowed his brow. "Another fall could set her back quite a ways."

HOW TO CARE FOR A LADY

"Oh, Evan, please," Lady Beeston said with a roll of her eyes. "That wasn't Dr. Alcott's fault."

The duke opened his mouth to retort, but he was cut off when his wife burst onto the verandah.

"There you are!" The duchess moved toward them, clad in a fetching day dress with an equally fetching bonnet upon her head, the ribbons of which she was attempting to tie with her gloved fingers. "We're going to be late."

The duke groaned, like a child might bemoan taking a bath.

"Oh, for heaven's sake, Evan, it's a garden party, not a tooth extraction."

"It might as well be," the duke groused.

Lady Beeston laughed, and it was quite infectious. All were giggling as Her Grace led her husband toward the door. All except the duke, of course.

"I guess he's not much for garden parties," Graham said as he moved around to the chair the duke had just vacated.

"What on earth would make you think that?" Lady Beeston teased back. "Poor man. He spent so many years hiding out in France, keeping his own council and without any obligation to anyone, I think it's rather overwhelming for him to be dragged about Town for balls and soirees and, of course, garden parties."

"And what of the duchess? She enjoys these things?

Lady Beeston burst into laughter. "Oh, my sister-in-law was quite born for these things, though she wasn't born *to* them."

"No?"

"Oh, no." The baroness shook her head. "Born into a farming family, believe it or not, but she had relations in the *ton,* a cousin at first, but then her sister married a Wetherby — you know the Wetherby family, of course?"

Everyone knew the Wetherby family. "Of course," he confirmed.

63

"And then her sister sponsored her in a season, and Grace, well...as you can imagine, she drew quite a bit of attention."

She was lovely—that was undeniable, and not at all objective. She had flaxen hair and wide eyes the color of emeralds, situated in a heart-shaped face. But Graham was much more drawn to the darker beauty that sat beside him.

Just now, little dots of the sunlight that streamed through the trees danced across her face so that she nearly sparkled, like some sort of fairy. She was utterly enchanting. Which was why Graham needed to be careful. Why he kept reminding himself that she was a patient, not a paramour.

Damn. He wouldn't know how to handle a paramour even if that were the case. He hadn't been with a woman in a very long time—his bachelor life had been too comfortable to compromise for a woman. But now, for the first time in his life, he thought he might not mind compromising his comfort.

"Then how did your brother come to meet her, if he wasn't one for soirees?" Graham wondered.

"Why, right over that garden wall." Lady Beeston cast her gaze to the right, to the wall that separated their property from that of the neighbors. "Her sister, Lady Chloe, lives there."

"Well, that is a lovely happenstance, isn't it?"

"Quite romantic, really." The baroness turned wistful as she looked out over the gardens. "I'm truly very happy for them, even if it is difficult to accept my own fate."

"You're only thirty, are you not?"

"I am," she said. "And widowed, quite scandalously, I might add. And crippled. I am quite damaged, Dr. Alcott."

Damaged or not, he was drawn to her in ways he couldn't describe. "You do yourself a disservice by thinking such things of yourself."

"I speak the truth."

"And yet, there are other perspectives to consider."

"Oh, really?" She turned her dark eyes on him. "Perhaps you can share them with me, for there is only one perspective from where I sit."

Graham swallowed and then cleared his throat. How much could he say without crossing that fine line between doctor and...something more?

TEN

Hannah didn't want to get her hopes high. He was her doctor. He was being paid to be encouraging. Surely, he was just being kind to help speed along her progress so he could move on to helping other patients.

And yet, the way he looked at her, like there was no one else in the world. Like he wanted to devour her—oh, goodness! There it was again, that insufferable heat that infused her every time she was embarrassed. Blast her shy nature. How often had she wished she were one of those formidable and unflappable women who could cut a man down with a sharp tongue and quick wit? She'd spent hours dreaming up such scenarios where she came out the victor, and then, when truly in the face of an odious man—her own husband included—she'd cowered and run away, only to shed enough tears to drown an entire ballroom full of people.

"If I may speak candidly," he finally said.

Hannah cleared her throat and nodded, unable to utter a single syllable.

"I think you are quite the most lovely woman I've ever had the pleasure of meeting." He turned in his chair, seeming emboldened all of a sudden. "Perhaps it isn't right for me to say so, but it's true, and I can't let you sit here and deprecate your good nature when I know better."

"But you hardly know me at all," she countered.

"I don't need to know you anymore than I already do to know what a good heart you have—what a good person you are. You love your family fiercely, and you have suffered with grace, that much I have deduced."

How he'd figured all that out in their short time together, she'd never know, and yet she couldn't disagree with him. Although, to say she'd suffered with grace might have been an overreaching statement. She'd certainly done her best, but Lord knew she'd had her weak moments.

"Do you know I fabricated a pregnancy when I was still married?" She wasn't certain why she felt compelled to tell him that all of a sudden. Perhaps she didn't want him to think *too* highly of her, lest he be disappointed down the line. Not that it mattered. She would likely reach a plateau in her progress and then there would be little need for his services.

His thin brows nearly touched his hair. "I beg your pardon?" There was the trace of a smile at the corners of his lips, and that caused a little giggle to bubble inside of Hannah.

She nodded, trying not to laugh. "It's true. It was a horrible thing to do, but..." A sigh escaped her as she sobered a bit. "I thought it would make things better. I thought he'd stop...well, stop doing what he was doing."

"I must admit, I'm quite surprised by this," Dr. Alcott said. "You seem so innocent, completely incapable of such a thing."

"And yet, I did it. So there. Not quite the saint you paint me to be, am I?"

He sat back in his chair, his eyes fixated on her, a grin fixed on his face. He crossed one long leg over the other. "If you think you are going to make me think less of you with stories from your past, you don't know me at all."

"Indeed, I know very little about you," she replied.

"Then perhaps we should remedy that."

Hannah's heart was racing all of a sudden. Whether it was from the doctor's attention so pointedly focused on her or the fact that she was more than ready for a rest, she couldn't be certain. Either way, she didn't have to say anything.

"But perhaps not today," Dr. Alcott said, scooting to the edge of his chair, his brow furrowed with concern. "How are you feeling?"

"A bit tired, is all," Hannah replied. "This has all been quite an adventure."

"There will be many more," he promised. "I will carry you up to bed and dress your wound before you sleep."

Hannah nodded gratefully just before he scooped her into his arms once more. It was quite a horrible thought, but part of her hoped she was never healed enough to actually walk again. She imagined she'd be fine having him carry her about everywhere instead. In spite of having such a long and lean appearance, he was rather strong beneath his coat. She could feel the band of muscles that supported her back, and the ones on his chest that currently pressed into her side. Why, he didn't even grunt or breathe heavier when he trekked up the stairs. It wasn't fair of her to compare him to her deceased husband, but truly, Beeston would have keeled over of a heart attack had he attempted to do something like this. He hadn't always been fat and weak, of course. He'd managed to carry her over the threshold on their wedding night. But that was the last time he ever carried her anywhere. Even the day he'd shot her, he'd been too beside himself to be of any use to anyone.

The memory of that day always made her stomach churn. What a stupid little fool she'd been, and for what? So what if Evan had shot the man dead? He was a duke—the magistrate wouldn't have been so hard on him, especially considering Beeston's reputation. But Hannah hadn't wanted to risk it. She didn't want anyone fighting on her behalf, and she certainly didn't want any bloodshed. Least of all, her own.

By the time they reached her room, Hannah's senses were all a whirl. She had no choice but to admit that she held a certain *tendre* for her doctor. It was innocent, of course. She could never act upon it. He was her doctor, after all. How scandalous that would be to abscond with her doctor in the wake of her husband taking his life. Still, she could hold him in high esteem, couldn't she? He was handsome and kind and intelligent, after all—a woman would have to be deaf, blind, and dumb not to feel the same way. But even then, it was his calming presence that spoke to her the most—that made her feel an easiness, a peacefulness that people rarely made her feel.

Of course, she loved her family, but they all had a way of draining her. Evan with his forceful air that practically shouted *I'm the duke!* Then Mother always looking down her nose at everything and everyone and exerting power, even when it wasn't her place. And Grace, who was so sweet and wonderful, and yet so very chatty and excitable. Yes, Dr. Alcott was the calm amidst the storm. Almost as much as that little bottle of laudanum was.

Which reminded her…

"Can you make certain my bottle of laudanum is replaced?" she asked as Dr. Alcott set her gently down on the bed. He stood over her, his brow still furrowed, his hazel eyes filled with concern. Hannah was starting to resent that look. She knew it meant he disapproved of her taking the stuff—that he knew she was taking more than she ought, blast it all. But she was in pain, and she needed sleep, didn't she? His poultice had helped the pain, but it hadn't calmed her nerves or put her to sleep like the laudanum did.

"I will ask that your maid administer the correct dosage throughout the day, but I don't think it wise to keep it here." He pointed to the nightstand.

"You may be my doctor, but you are not in charge of me. I am a grown woman, and I can make my own decisions."

"Your decisions could lead to a dependency that you become helpless to. I've seen it too many times to let it happen to you."

On the one hand, she was touched that he cared enough to not let her waste her life away to laudanum. On the other hand, she knew she'd never sleep again without it. "You are being quite boorish," she said, regretting the words almost as soon as they were out of her mouth. But if Dr. Alcott was hurt by them, he didn't indicate as much. As a matter of fact, he gave a little laugh.

"If that is how you think of me for protecting your health, then there is nothing for it. I will be as boorish as an army general if I must be."

Hannah was angry. And at the same time quite moved by his concern. Not that she was going to tell *him* that. She wanted her laudanum, and she wanted it now. No matter how kind and thoughtful he was being toward her, she would put up a fight until he gave in.

"And I shall match your boorishness with obstinacy." Much to her frustration, he was grinning to himself, as if he had some secret about her that was so very humorous. "What are you laughing about?"

"Oh, nothing," he said, attempting to school his features into a more somber expression...and failing miserably.

"You're making fun of me," she pouted. And really, it wasn't like her to be like this, all pouty and obtuse, but she couldn't help herself. He seemed to alternately bring out the best and the worst in her.

Well, perhaps not the worst. Beeston had done that. He'd made her meek and afraid and guilt-ridden—being petulant was far better than that, wasn't it?

"Never," Dr. Alcott replied, and his voice had dropped to something low and sincere that made Hannah flush all over. "Tease you, perhaps. But never make fun."

"Oh," she said, for really, she couldn't think of anything else at all to say.

Their eyes were locked—she was completely lost in his hazel depths, in the way they caught the light from the window, making them so green and mesmerizing. Her heart raced, and she found it hard to catch her breath, which was why she ultimately turned away, gasping for air.

Dr. Alcott set to work readying the poultice, and Hannah pulled her nightrail up until her wound, covered in the large, white bandage, was revealed. The air was cool on her leg, and something inside her stirred. Longing. A desire for him to caress her bare leg. To hold her gaze again. To crawl into the bed with her and stay from dusk until dawn. She was being ridiculous and fanciful, but she couldn't seem to stop herself.

"Everything all right?" he asked, pulling her out of her romantic reverie as he removed yesterday's bandage, revealing the hole in her leg.

"Goodness, that looks much improved, doesn't it?" she remarked, quite taken aback that the wound wasn't as red and festering as it had been a few days ago. "What in the world is in that poultice?"

"A great many things," the doctor said as he pressed the moistened cloth to her leg. It stung, but not as badly as the day before. "But of all the ingredients, it is my belief that the Frankincense is the most beneficial. It is the most rare and most expensive. But, of course, all the oils and herbs are working toge—

My lady?"

Hannah popped her head up to look at him, only just then realizing she'd reached up to touch his shoulder. *Dear God.*

"I'm sorry," she said, stuttering over the simple words and flushing to what she was certain was a tomato-like color. How utterly humiliating. "I didn't mean...that is, I was just..."

"You needn't apologize."

He was staring at her again, gazing right into her eyes, down into her very soul. She wasn't in her right mind, not with him so close and her leg so bare. This went far beyond propriety into downright scandalous behavior.

She ought to say something else—something to break the tension that hung so palpably in the room—but she couldn't think of a word to say. At least, not an appropriate word to say. *Kiss me* was most definitely not appropriate. And yet, it was what she wanted. To feel his lips on hers, his lean body pressed against her. To run her fingers through his head of sand-colored hair. How she longed for intimacy, and not with just any man, but with Dr. Alcott. Only he would do.

Blessedly, he saved her from having to say anything more when he turned back to his black leather bag and began to pack his things away. "I do think this was a success, don't you?" he asked, and it was as if that awkward and charged moment had never happened. "You must be tired though, now."

In truth, she was wound tighter than a brand new pocket watch. "I should probably rest," she agreed. "I will see you tomorrow?"

He turned his perfectly handsome and kind face to her. "And every day until you are well enough to do without me."

Then I shall never get well.

ELEVEN

The following days tending to Lady Beeston were some of the most difficult of Graham's professional life. After she'd touched his shoulder, with her gentle hand, so absently, as if it were the most natural thing in the world, well...Graham had struggled to maintain his professionalism. Thankfully, her family had been quite involved, all of them in and out of the baroness's chambers, never once leaving them alone. And on their trips to and from the gardens, for her ladyship felt the fresh air was quite instrumental in her progress, her brother had carried her up and down the stairs. Graham wondered if perhaps Lady Beeston had said something to them about their meaningful glances and obvious attraction, but not a one of them seemed to treat him any differently. Surely, the young duchess would find it hard not to grin and giggle at him, or the duke not to scowl at him menacingly, or the dowager to keep her mouth shut on the matter. Surely, she would never approve of her daughter, daughter of the Duke of Somerset and titled as a baroness, falling in love with a doctor.

Graham shook his head. *In love*? That was a bit far-fetched, wasn't it? Goodness, he was becoming quite fanciful. Even Daphne would laugh in his face for such a notion.

"Graham, is that you?"

Speaking of his sister... "Good morning," he greeted her. She was looking quite lovely this morning—the glow of motherhood high in her cheeks. "You have quite a glow about you today."

"That, dear brother, is sweat," she corrected. Then she snapped open her fan as she plopped onto a nearby settee. "But tell me, what brings you this way?"

Graham sat down in yellow wing-backed chair. "I was hoping to ask a favor of you."

73

Daphne continued to fan herself. "Perhaps you could open a window before you do. Some cool air might make me more inclined to say yes."

Graham laughed as he did her bidding. "Better?" he asked as a cool breeze wafted into the room. Thank heaven it wasn't terribly hot today, as August could tend to be.

"Much. Now, go on. What is this favor?"

"Well," Graham said, taking his seat again. "I wonder if you might call on a friend of mine today."

Daphne raised her brows at him. "You have friends?"

"Admittedly, not many, but yes, I do," he replied pointedly.

"I hardly think it would be appropriate for me to call on one of your doctor friends."

"But it isn't a doctor," he corrected. "It's a woman."

He let the word hang in the air. It would only be a matter of seconds...

"A woman?" Daphne shot up on the settee, her bright blue eyes suddenly filled with interest.

"A patient," he amended.

"Go on."

"Lady Beeston, to be precise."

Now Daphne's eyes, already round of nature, widened even more. It was the same look their mother used to give their father when he said something surprising, like to report that a young woman was pregnant out of wedlock or that a man in his prime had been struck by an attack of the heart. It was in little moments like this that he missed his parents and wondered what his life would be like if they hadn't perished in that fire.

"Oh, yes!" Daphne said, clearly remembering their conversation of last week. "How is she faring?"

"Better," he said, feeling rather proud of himself. "I'm quite pleased to say my treatments are working."

A small smile spread Daphne's lips. "Oh, if only Father were here to see you."

"Do you not believe he is looking down on us? Watching from above?"

"I like to believe that. But it would be nice to hear their voices again, wouldn't it? To know that they're happy with the choices we've made."

"I've no doubt they'd be very proud of the Viscountess Wolverly."

"And the grand London doctor."

They laughed and then fell silent.

"So, will you go?" he asked.

"Are you certain she's receiving visitors?"

Graham nodded. "It is part of her treatment, but I don't want to overwhelm her. Someone who knows and understands the situation is ideal. You'll hardly be put out if she wilts like a flower and needs to go back to bed."

"Of course," Daphne said. "I will be agreeable, and I'll even bring some rum butter. That ought to cheer her sufficiently, don't you think?"

"Indeed." Graham patted his belly, thinking of the delicious spread. If there was any fat on his body it was entirely due to far too much rum butter in his diet. "Tomorrow, then?"

"I'd be delighted."

~*~

"Are you certain I'm ready for this?"

Lady Beeston stood by the bed—actually *stood!*—holding onto one of the four posters. She was dressed in a lavender day gown, her hair gathered into a simple, loose chignon at her nape. Her cheeks were rosy, her lips pink, her eyes bright. She was like a different woman from the one he'd first visited a couple weeks ago, and Graham couldn't help but be proud of what he'd accomplished with her. She claimed the pain was quite minimal now, and he was successfully weaning her off the laudanum, day by day, reducing the dose by a tiny bit. So little, in fact, it seemed she didn't even notice.

"If you're not, remember, it is only my sister," he said to her, unable to keep the smile from his lips. She was radiant, like a ray of sunshine in his life.

"And she knows about all of this?" she confirmed for the hundredth time.

He nodded. "She knows enough. Now, come. I will escort you down."

She took his arm—it was all the support she needed these days to get around. She was even navigating the stairs, slowly, of course, but traversing them nonetheless.

They arrived in the drawing room where the duchess and the dowager both awaited them. The younger of the two leapt from her seat and bounded to them, taking Lady Beeston's arm.

"Look at you," Her Grace cried, tears of joy shimmering in her eyes. "And here we thought you'd never walk again."

Lady Beeston cast a sweet glance toward Graham, her coquettish smile setting his heart to racing. "We all have Dr. Alcott to thank for my quick recovery."

"Oh, indeed!" the duchess agreed. "You've worked miracles, Doctor."

"He got lucky," the dowager put in from her perch across the room. The high-back chair might as well have been a throne.

But Graham was coming to enjoy the old woman's biting sense of humor, though she certainly didn't think of her words as a joke. Still, he couldn't help but laugh at her.

"Well, either way," he said, "I'm quite happy with Lady Beeston's progress."

"Lady Wolverly," came the dry tone of the Somerset butler.

All eyes turned to the doorway where his sister stood, decked out in the finest fripperies money could buy. She had really grown quite accustomed to life as an aristocrat, considering her humble beginnings.

The duchess was the first to greet her, leaving Lady Beeston alone with Graham once again.

"Lady Wolverly, how delighted we are to have you for tea today," she said, sweeping about the room with all the grace that both her name and title implied. "Do come have a seat. Dr. Alcott, if you would please settle Lady Beeston here." She indicated a chair at the small round table, and Graham led his patient directly to it, as his sister and the duchess took their own seats.

"But there are only four chairs," Lady Beeston said to her sister-in-law.

"That is quite all right," Graham replied, as the baroness turned her lovely dark eyes to him. "I will make myself comfortable elsewhere until you're finished."

"Oh." Lady Beeston blinked at him, her eyes somewhat pleading. She wanted him to stay, though why, he couldn't exactly say. She had her mother and sister-in-law to tend to her for the time being. "All right, then. Thank you, Dr. Alcott."

She held his gaze until he finally broke away and left the room.

~*~

Hannah had grown quite accustomed to having Dr. Alcott at her side, so it was quite unnerving that he was *not* in this present moment. Her mother offered little comfort, and Grace was like a whirling dervish, chattering away as she prepared the tea.

"Will you stay in town for Christmas?" she asked of the viscountess. "Or will you go back to...where is it again? Cumberland?"

Lady Wolverly nodded. "Indeed. A little town called Ravenglass. You may know it for the infamous Marisdùn Castle."

Grace gasped. "I *have* heard of that place! Tell me, have you been inside?"

77

The viscountess laughed. "Too many times to count, now. Why, Marisdùn was quite instrumental in my meeting of Lord Wolverly."

"Is that so?" Grace leaned forward, enrapt.

"He was staying there with friends, and he'd come to find the doctor. Graham wasn't at home, so I went instead, covered in...Oh! That reminds me!" She reached into her oversized reticule and pulled out a small jar of what looked like caramel. "I brought this for you. Cumberland Rum Butter—I was quite known for it in Ravenglass."

"And you are quite known for it here, too!" Grace added. "Why, Lady Pevanshire served this at tea the other day, and all the ladies simply raved over it. Goodness, I didn't even put it all together. May we open it? How do you think it will taste with this?" She cut into the small white cake that sat directly before her on the table.

"There is only one way to find out," the dowager said, and Hannah granted herself a small smile over her mother's sweet tooth. Her stoic exterior was compromised only in the face of dessert.

"Lady Beeston..." The viscountess turned her stunning blue eyes on her as Grace served up slices of cake covered in rum butter. "How are you feeling? I do hope this isn't too taxing for you."

"On the contrary," Hannah said, thinking she quite liked the viscountess. She was closer to her in age than Grace was— not that she didn't love Grace, but her sister-in-law still lacked in maturity sometimes. Of course, what she lacked, her sister, Chloe, made up for in spades. She likely came out of the womb knowing how to tend to the house and the children—just the sort of woman Lord Andrew Wetherby had needed, being a known rogue before he'd met her. Quite the scrapes he and his twin had gotten into in their younger days. But now they were both happily settled, Andrew with a brood of children himself. "I'm feeling quite invigorated, and I daresay the rum butter and cake will be quite a boon."

HOW TO CARE FOR A LADY

"I do hope so," Lady Wolverly said, just before they all fell silent and took their first bite of the dessert.

It was heavenly. Cook had outdone herself with the cake today, but the rum butter was the perfect compliment. Sweet and spicy and buttery—Hannah was certain she'd never be able to have cake without it again.

"I only realized I never answered your question," the viscountess said after they'd all had a few more bites. "I do believe we will stay in the city through the holidays, actually. I find it much more lively than being cooped up in the country. And what about you?"

Grace sighed. "Christmas in the city does sound wonderful, but I'm afraid I'll be in confinement by then, so we will all head to the family seat in Sussex."

"Many congratulations," the viscountess said. "Children are indeed a joy."

Mother cleared her throat, clearly uncomfortable with the way the conversation had steered. Whether it was because she hadn't enjoyed being a mother or because she thought the topic of childbearing inappropriate over tea, Hannah couldn't be certain. Perhaps a combination of the two?

"Well, I, for one, would much prefer to stay here," Mother said. "Lady Wolverly is right. It is much more lively in the city."

"What would *you* prefer?" the viscountess asked, turning to Hannah.

Hannah hadn't given it much thought. For a long time, she'd assumed she'd never go anywhere but her bedchamber again. But now she considered it... "Beeston always wanted to be in the city for Christmas. The divertissements around Town are only as fun as the people you're with—since I was alone, well... I suppose I could enjoy the city if I had friends to enjoy it with. But Christmas in the country sounds very quaint, don't you think?"

"I could do without quaint," Grace put in. "That's all I ever knew until recently."

"They do say the grass is always greener on the other side of the street." Mother took another sip of tea.

"Lady Beeston," the viscountess said, training her blue eyes on her. "I know you are still recovering, but I'm hoping to host a little soiree in a few weeks time, at the start of the Little Season. I know you are still in mourning, but I promise it will be small—not much more than a family gathering. If you are well enough, I would very much like to see you there—and your family too, of course."

"Oh." Hannah looked to her sister-in-law, then her mother, and finally back to Lady Wolverly. "I, um…I haven't been out in public yet. Is it even proper for me to do so?"

"I hardly think anyone will fault you under the circumstances," Grace put in. "And besides, she says it's not much more than a family dinner."

The viscountess laid her hand atop Hannah's. "You needn't decide now. Invitations will go out next week—you can decide then. But even at that, I won't think less of you should you bow out at the last minute."

"I suppose you can put me down as a definite maybe then," Hannah said, and they all laughed.

"Wonderful," Lady Wolverly said. "I fear I must be going now, but I do so look forward to seeing you all again."

"Likewise," Hannah said, and then she was left alone with her mother while Grace saw the viscountess to the door.

"You're looking a bit peaked, Hannah," Mother pointed out, as if Hannah didn't know.

"Yes, I'm certain I do. Perhaps you can call Dr. Alcott to retrieve me?" She would feel much better with him by her side.

Mother hesitated for a long moment. The way she stared at her, in silent judgment, made Hannah uneasy. Did she suspect something? Did she see in her eyes, or in his, the high regard they held for one another. To be truthful, it was getting harder and harder to hide her feelings from him. In part, he was like her savior, nursing her back to health and bringing light into her life after so many dark years. But beyond that, he was a good person, a kind person. So easy to talk to and to be around. Just being near him set her at ease in a way she'd not been for so very long.

"Yes, of course," Mother finally said, and then she removed herself from the room.

Moments later, she returned, Dr. Alcott trailing behind her, stealing Hannah's breath away. Was it possible he was even more handsome now than he'd been just a half hour ago when he'd deposited her here? Or perhaps it was just the smile he wore—like it was only for her—like he was truly happy to see her again.

"So?" he asked as he approached the table and Mother took her seat. "How was tea?"

"Your sister is delightful," Hannah said, beaming up at him. "And her rum butter—"

"Is divine," Mother cut her off.

"Mother has a sweet tooth to rival even the most greedy of children."

Mother sucked in a sharp breath and let it out slowly, shaking her head. "It is true, I'm afraid. But now I need to lie down. Dr. Alcott, you can see to my daughter?"

"She is in good hands, Your Grace."

Mother left the room again, her black skirts swishing loudly on her way out. Hannah looked up at Dr. Alcott, who towered above her, losing herself in his shimmering hazel eyes.

"My lady?" he said, extending his hand to her. She took it, the strength and warmth sending shockwaves through her, and he pulled her easily from the chair.

"Thank you," she said as they began the slow walk toward the door. "Your sister really is lovely. And she's invited us to her home for a party in a few weeks."

"Has she now?"

Hannah looked sideways at him to see he wore a mischievous half smile. "I don't suppose you had anything to do with it, did you?"

81

"Me?" he asked, all innocence. "I can't imagine what purpose I would have in encouraging such a thing."

Hannah suddenly felt ridiculous. She supposed there was a part of her that hoped he had put Lady Wolverly up to it. Perhaps as a way to attend a social function with her—maybe dance a slow waltz together or take a stroll out to the verandah. But of course she was only being fanciful. She was in mourning, for heaven's sake. She shouldn't be going out at all, let alone engaging in waltzes and flirtations.

"But," he continued as they began the slow ascent up the stairs, "if you are going, I suppose I should be there too. You know, to keep an eye on you and make certain you don't need medical attention."

And then he winked at her. Goodness! He *had* orchestrated it! And here he was flirting with her. At least, she thought he was. It had been far too long since she'd flirted, she wasn't certain she'd know it if it smacked her across the face.

"Oh, yes," she replied, playing along. "Medical attention."

"Indeed."

TWELVE

Graham was feeling quite proud of himself. The past weeks had proven to be highly successful in terms of his patient, and just the day before, she'd hobbled down the stairs and to the gardens without any assistance at all from him. She still needed to use the banister or the walls to keep steady but was otherwise quite independent.

Part of Graham was thrilled by this, while part of him missed being able to put his arms about her waist and hold her close. Close enough to smell the rosewater she'd rinsed her hair with, or the bespoke perfume she wore, something with orange blossoms and cinnamon, he thought. Whatever it was, it drove him mad and made him wish desperately that they could be more than just doctor and patient.

To that end, he'd become more bold, flirting openly with her and reveling in the fact that she was flirting with him in return. It was unlikely, completely far fetched, but he hoped that he might share his feelings at his sister's soiree and, with any luck, have them returned.

Said soiree was fast approaching, and Graham was spending many an hour before the mirror in his bedchamber, practicing his speech to her. *Hannah.* Oh, how he longed to call her by her Christian name, and to have her do the same. To hear his name on her lips would surely be transcendent. Goodness, he wasn't usually so fanciful. He was a man of science. And yet, he couldn't seem to help himself when it came to Lady Beeston.

A knock came at his door, pulling him from his own reflection. He made his way to the front door and opened it to reveal a messenger boy.

"Are you Dr. Alcott?" the boy asked.

"I am."

The boy held out a letter, and Graham dropped a coin into his hand before he ran off to find his next assignment. Graham studied the outside of the letter—there was no mistaking Dr. Pritchard's scrawled handwriting. Barely legible, it was a wonder it had made it here.

Uneasiness settled in his belly as he tore at the seal, but he discovered that his worry was unfounded once he began to read.

Dr. Alcott,

Word of Lady Beeston's speedy recovery has spread so fast and so far that it has already reached me here in the country. I needn't go on about how proud I am, for surely you are quite proud of yourself. Keep up the good work, my good man. If all goes well here, I shall be back in the city before the Little Season ends. I look forward to sharing a meal with you at the club upon my return.

Please send my regards to Lady Beeston and her family, and my best to you.

Your friend,

Dr. Pritchard

Graham smiled as he tucked the letter into his desk drawer and then glanced outside to see a perfectly sunny day beyond the windows. He had an idea all of a sudden.

Cravat nicely in place and a spring in his step, he left his apartments and set out for Bond Street. The weather was cooling as they approached the autumn, and the leaves were beginning to change their colors. The city was aglow in reds and oranges and yellows, and Graham realized, for the first time since he'd come to London seven years ago, that it was a rather magical time of year. Pity he'd not noticed before. It seemed Lady Beeston had awakened something within him— something that made him appreciate the lovely, beautiful world in which they lived.

He went straight to *Babbock's Fine Accoutrements for Gentlemen*, where he bought all his own accoutrements. Mr.

HOW TO CARE FOR A LADY

Babbock was there to greet him with a gentle smile, ready to assist.

"Dr. Alcott," he said, as Graham entered the shop. "A pleasure, sir. What brings you in today? All out of handkerchiefs again?"

Graham gave a little laugh, for he had a habit of either lending or losing his handkerchiefs. "No, no," he replied. "Soon, but not today. I'm actually looking for something quite special."

"Indeed?" The proprietor raised his brows, all intrigue. "Go on."

"A walking stick."

"A walking stick?" The intrigue seemed to have died.

"For a woman — a patient, that is."

"Ah!" There was a question in the older man's dark blue eyes, but he held his tongue and led Graham to the display of walking sticks along the far wall.

Graham examined each one, contemplating the wood and the metal work on the handle, but all of them rang far too masculine for Lady Beeston. She was a strong woman, yes, but so very feminine at the same time. It needed to be something that reflected that about her.

"Do you see anything you like?" Mr. Babbock asked after a while.

Graham shook his head. "None of them are quite right."

"Perhaps you want to commission a bespoke walking stick for your...patient."

It would cost him quite a bit more, but he wasn't exactly in the poorhouse. He could afford this small luxury, even if it wasn't for himself. "Tell me, can it be ready by next Wednesday? I would like to present it before then."

Mr. Babbock nodded. "I don't see why that would be a problem. Come to my office and we shall design it together."

~*~

It seemed unreal. Like a wonderful dream come true. She was walking again — well, hobbling — without assistance of

85

any kind. If one didn't count the walls and railings, that was. But she didn't. And she was immensely proud of herself. And she was equally grateful for Dr. Alcott. His concoction of oils and herbs had done wonders for the wound, and she was all but done with laudanum. How addled her brain had been by the stuff! Sure, she had moments of weakness when she couldn't sleep still, but Dr. Alcott had encouraged her to use that time to write in her journal or read a book rather than succumb to the laudanum.

Hannah took a deep breath of the fresh air as she emerged onto the verandah. It was crisp and sunny out, and she felt so very alive. So very happy.

Of course, she'd be even happier when Dr. Alcott arrived. The line between patient and friend was blurring more and more every day. As she healed, her need for his services was dwindling, but her desire for his friendship—or something more—was growing by leaps and bounds.

"Oh, Evan!" she said, heading toward her usual spot at the far end of the verandah. "I didn't expect to find you out here."

Her brother dropped the paper he'd been reading and smiled up at her as she limped along the wall toward him. "Well, good morning, Bunny," he said, straightening in his chair. "Have you broken your fast yet?"

"Not yet," she admitted. "But I've already instructed Alice to have my breakfast brought out here. How is Grace? I haven't seen much of her lately."

"My wife," he began, "is not feeling herself, I'm afraid."

"Oh, dear." Hannah had heard how pregnancy could affect one's state. It didn't sound fun at all, and yet, she'd give anything to experience it. "The baby?"

Evan nodded, a piece of his dark hair falling over one eye. "It's terrible, really. Tossing up her accounts at all hours of the day."

How to Care for a Lady

"Funny how fast it came on. She was fine just a couple weeks ago, having tea and going to garden parties. Is it normal?"

"How should I know?" Evan shrugged.

"Perhaps Dr. Alcott could look after her, what with Dr. Pritchard being away."

"I would hate to take his focus away from you when you're doing so well."

"My need for him is dwindling." *Unfortunately.* "I think I can spare him to examine Grace once in a while and make certain all is coming along as it should with the baby."

Evan glanced up at her. "You're certain?"

"More than certain." Besides, if Dr. Alcott was seeing to Grace throughout her pregnancy, that would guarantee another seven months or so of his presence in their home, even if Hannah didn't need him anymore. She'd not say no to that.

"I will speak to him when he arrives then." Evan gestured toward somewhere behind Hannah. "Here comes your breakfast now. I will leave you to it while I go to check on Grace."

"Please ask if I may visit her later on, won't you? I've quite missed her company."

Evan leaned down to place a kiss on her cheek. "I will indeed."

Hannah tucked into her meal, which consisted of eggs, bacon and sweet biscuits with a side of rum butter. She'd managed to find a way to incorporate Lady Wolverly's delectable rum butter into almost every meal lately. Between herself and her mother, the stuff would be gone soon. She made a mental note to order more jars just as Dr. Alcott walked through the doors onto the verandah. He looked especially happy today, and that, in turn, made Hannah happy.

"I was wondering how long I'd have to wait to see you this morning," she said as he approached. They'd become quite bold and quite familiar lately, and it warmed Hannah's heart. *This* was what she'd always longed for with Beeston.

87

Friendship. Laughter. Long conversations and challenging discourse. Of course, all she'd gotten was indifference for ten long years.

"Well, your wait is over, my lady," he said as he took a seat at the table across from her. "I didn't expect to find you down here, though. Did anyone help you from your room?"

Hannah smiled proudly and shook her head. "No. I did it all by myself."

"I see you're quite proud of that fact," he said. "But I'd rather you have someone with you...just in case."

"Your concern is heartwarming, but as you can see, I made it here just fine."

"Still..."

"I've just been talking with Somerset," she went on, not allowing him to crush her good mood with his over-cautiousness. "My sister-in-law is having quite a time with the babe."

Dr. Alcott's dark brows knitted together. "I was hoping Her Grace had avoided morning sickness."

"Oh, it's not just the morning, you know? Somerset says it's all day. We've both agreed we'd like to have you look after her during the pregnancy, but of course, he will speak to you himself."

"I would be more than happy to, but Dr. Pritchard will be back soon. Wouldn't the duchess prefer to be under his care?"

Hannah blinked up at him. "I don't see why. He left me in *your* care, and quite frankly, I'm glad he did." Her heart was racing now. There were things she wanted to say—things that shouldn't be expressed from patient to doctor—but somehow she just couldn't help herself. "It hasn't all been fun, but I would say that the last couple months have been..." She swallowed. Could she say it? Could she open the door that might lead to more? "Well, they have been the best months of my life."

She was shaking. Like a leaf about to break free of its branch. Why wasn't he saying anything? Why did he just sit there, staring at her? She couldn't stand it. Hadn't she, in some way, just confessed her feelings for him? And there he sat, saying *nothing*.

"Aren't you going to say something?" she asked, terrified that his answer was going to be something she didn't want to hear.

And then, just when she was about to excuse herself out of embarrassment, a smile broke out on his lips, lighting his eyes as his gaze bore into her.

"To be truthful, I would rather not *say* anything."

Oh, of course. He was laughing at her. How could she have misread the signs? How could she have mistaken his kindness for flirtation? What a fool she was! And if she excused herself, it would be even more awkward, for she walked so slowly, and then, of course, he'd want to assist her...

"Hannah," he said, and his tone was so soft, so gentle, that it immediately quieted her whirling thoughts.

"Yes?" she replied, her body tingling from hearing her Christian name on his lips.

"They have been the best months of *my* life, too."

THIRTEEN

"Really?" The word came out so quietly that he barely heard it.

"Yes," he confirmed, feeling emboldened now that she'd come out with her own feelings. He moved to the edge of his chair, putting him that much closer to her. "Is it all right that I call you Hannah?"

"More than all right." Her smile beamed from ear to ear. "But am I to continue to call you Dr. Alcott?"

He took hold of her hand. They had touched many times in the past months, but this was different. This was not doctor to patient, this was human to human. And dare he hope, lover to lover? There was so much promise in this simple gesture of holding hands, and it took all of Graham's willpower to keep from exploring those unspoken promises.

"I would be honored if you would call me Graham."

"Graham," she whispered, as if it were a prayer. Then she swallowed, her slender throat working, her brows coming together in a frown. "What does this all mean?"

Graham had no idea. "I've never fallen in love with a patient before," he said, making her frown fall away in favor of a laugh.

"I'm very glad for that."

"But if you're asking where we go from here, I really don't know. I can't imagine your family will be thrilled to hear that we…"

"Care for one another?"

It was all Graham could do not to sweep her into his arms and kiss her until she forgot her own name just then. How could her husband not have seen what a lovely creature she was? How could he have treated her so poorly, this beautiful angel that sat before him? It was unfathomable that anyone would ever take advantage of her, and Graham swore no one ever would again. He would be her protector from now on, and she'd never come to any harm so long as he was alive.

"Care for one another," he confirmed.

Hannah closed her eyes. There was a smile on her lips, but one couldn't miss the tiny tear that eked from between her eyelids.

"Do not cry, dear one," Graham whispered, reaching across the divide with his other hand to wipe the tear from her cheek.

"I—I've wanted to say something to you for so long."

"And I *you*."

"But you're right," she continued. "What will my family say?"

"I suspect this will be challenging territory." He took both her hands now and squeezed. "But we will navigate it together, if you will have me."

She gave a snort of laughter through her tears. "Of course I will have you. But we may want to consider elopement."

"No." He was happy to give her just about anything to make her happy but that was not one of them.

"No?" She batted her lashes at him, her eyes wide as a young doe.

"I want to marry you," he said, making certain he was clear on that point, though saying it aloud was somewhat terrifying, if he was being honest. "But I'll not do it in secrecy, as if we have something to hide."

"But the scandal..."

"Is of no consequence to me," he finished for her. "I want our families to be there. I know how much yours means to you, and there is no one more precious to me in this world than my sister." He quirked a smile. "Although, there is someone who may offer a challenge to that position."

Hannah gave a little laugh, and squeezed his hands that were still entwined with hers. "I suppose the news would reach the gossips either way, wouldn't it? What with Chloe being a Wetherby and all. News travels fast with that family."

"Then it is settled." He started to pull away—he was so full of excited energy, he needed to stand or walk or run to Surrey and back—but Hannah kept him still.

"Wait," she said, meeting his eyes with a sober plea in her own. "Might we keep this a secret? Just for a little while," she added to reassure him. "This is all so...new, and I just want to savor it for a bit before the rest of the world starts offering their opinions on the matter."

Graham supposed it was all moving rather too quickly anyway. In a normal situation, he would court her for several months before offering for her hand and then there would be several more weeks or even months of waiting before they married. Of course, they'd have to have the banns read, so that would take time, but he could see the logic in her request. It would be nice to have this secret between the two of them. Besides, surely the dowager wouldn't allow them to be alone if there was any sign of affection between them. Perhaps they could take advantage of their current situation.

"I think that is a wise idea," he finally replied. "What if we were to announce our engagement at my sister's soiree? It will be a small gathering, mostly family and close friends. I can think of no better time to make such an announcement."

That serene smile he loved so much graced Hannah's lips. "I think that is a wonderful idea."

The breeze lifted a strand of her mahogany hair just as he lifted her hand to his mouth. He closed his eyes as he pressed his lips to her soft skin, lingering far longer than he should.

"Ho, there! Dr. Alcott!" came the boisterous greeting of the duke from somewhere behind him.

Hannah's face flushed pink, but Graham kept his calm, holding onto her hand and offering a wink to reassure her.

HOW TO CARE FOR A LADY

"Your pulse is just fine," he said, slowly lowering her hand back to her lap just before he turned to greet his future brother-in-law. "Your Grace."

"Everything all right?" he asked, his eyes narrowed on Graham.

"Just checking her pulse. I wanted to make certain she wasn't taxing herself by being out here."

Somerset took a seat. "Her progress is remarkable, Doctor. I feel horrible I ever doubted you."

"It is not the first time I have been challenged, and I don't imagine it will be the last."

"Well, not from me, ever again," Somerset said. "Which leads me to my next question…"

"I've already told him," Hannah put in. "And he says he is happy to care for Grace."

Somerset turned his ice-blue gaze on Graham. "Is that true?"

"You think I would lie?" Hannah interrupted.

"May I speak with the doctor myself, Bunny?" he asked of his sister then turned to Graham again. Graham couldn't help the laugh that escaped him. He was no stranger to sibling spats, and knowing other siblings had similar arguments was somewhat comforting.

"Your sister is correct," Graham finally put in. "I would be happy to be of service. Should I see to her now?"

"That's a wonderful idea," Hannah said. "Poor girl has been suffering so. Perhaps you can ease her suffering as you've done mine."

Any fool could see the loving way she looked at him, with admiration and adoration in her eyes. If she wanted to keep things a secret, she wasn't doing a very good job of it. Of course, he probably wasn't either. He only need glance at her to feel his heart lift along with the corners of his lips.

"I will endeavor to do my best," he replied, lingering in her gaze.

93

"Well, then," Somerset said, giving two loud knocks on the garden table, "I shall lead the way. Are you all right for now, Bunny?"

"I'm fine," she assured her brother. "I shall sit here and read for a while."

As much as Graham wanted to stay by her side and hold her hands all afternoon, he also felt the familiar excitement of seeing to a new patient. The anticipation of helping someone find their way back to good health. So he dutifully followed Somerset through the house to the ducal chambers on the second floor.

"I will warn you," the duke said as they approached the door. "She is quite ill."

"It is not so unusual for a woman in her position," Graham assured the man. "Another few weeks and she should be right as rain. But hopefully I can do something to ease her ailments in the meantime."

The duke nodded and then opened the door quietly. It was dark inside and smelled of sickness—much like Hannah's room had smelled that first day he'd come to meet her. How much had changed in such a short amount of time.

A small figure writhed upon the bed, covered in blankets. Graham went to her and placed a hand on her back. She groaned but didn't settle.

"Darling," the duke said, approaching the other side of the bed. "Dr. Alcott is here to see you."

There was a small whimper, and then, "Can you help me?"

Graham smiled. "I can try," he said. "Tell me what you're feeling."

"Like I..." She put her hand to her mouth. "Like I can't get through a sentence without..."

Graham reached for the chamber pot and held it out for her while she heaved into it.

"Have you been able to eat anything?"

She shook her head no.

"Drink anything?"

No again.

"All right. We must first settle your stomach so that you can keep food and drink in, lest you become dehydrated. You may still feel ill, perhaps for a few more weeks, but that is completely normal."

"This is torture," she whimpered as she lifted her teary eyes to him.

"So I've heard. But you will be fine. I will return shortly with tea and bread."

He settled her back onto her pillows and then left to instruct Cook on how to prepare a tea of ginger and peppermint for Her Grace. Once he had the nourishments in hand, he headed back toward the ducal chambers. He was halfway up the first staircase when a sweet and familiar voice called out for him.

"Dr. Alcott," said the voice, and when he turned to find Hannah standing behind him, clutching the banister, she gave him a wink. "How is my sister-in-law?"

He descended the steps again, until he stood just over her. Light from the fanlight poured into the room, shining upon her dark hair as if she truly wore a halo above her head. The urge to kiss her was stronger than ever, but this was neither the time nor the place. "She is as expected. Quite nauseous, unable to keep food down."

Hannah's lovely, dark brows drew together with concern. "Will she and the babe be all right?"

Graham nodded, giving what he hoped was a reassuring smile, and gestured to the tray he held in his hands. "Once she's had this, they will be."

While concern still marred her brow, she gave him a smile in return, touching her hand to his arm. "Thank you," she said. "And, erm...if you would come see me after you've seen to Grace, I do believe my leg needs tending to."

Everything in her tone and in her eyes told him her leg was just fine, but he would go to her, nonetheless.

FOURTEEN

She was mad. There was no other explanation. Had she really invited him to her room with a fib and a seductive wink? Goodness, she was a harridan, a harlot! She had never done anything like this, not even in the early days with Beeston. He had been so pursuant of her, she hadn't needed to. But this was different. She wasn't an innocent this time. Dr. Alcott—*Graham*—wasn't a powerful lord that put stars in her eyes and clouded her judgment.

No, this was far more special. There was friendship and tenderness and...everything that wasn't there with Beeston.

Damn Beeston! Why was she thinking of him at a time like this? Why did his memory choose to creep up and strangle her just when happiness was within her grasp?

"Hannah?"

Hannah whirled, her heart racing, to find Dr. Alcott behind her. Graham. Blast, it would take time to get used to calling him by his given name.

"I didn't hear you come in," she said, clutching her hand to her chest. How had he opened and closed the door without her knowing?

"Did I startle you?"

He had, but that wasn't why her heart was racing. "I'm fine," she breathed, her eyes locked with his. The air in the room heavy. The charge of passion palpable between them, drawing them together, an unseen force that neither could deny.

And then, before she could even form another thought, she was in his arms. His mouth was on hers, coaxing her lips apart until she gave in, allowing his tongue entry, mingling with her own. Every nerve in her body stood on end, heat flooded her to her core. His hands, so familiar to her now as her doctor, held her so tenderly, caressed her so gently, and she melted against him. She'd been waiting for this for so many weeks now. No, years. She'd dreamt of this kind of passion often during her disappointing marriage, but she never could have imagined how wonderful it would truly be to be held. To be loved.

"My darling," Graham whispered—it was easy to think of him as Graham all of a sudden, for who could consider their doctor doing *this* to them? "Are those tears?"

Hannah reached up to touch her cheek, which was indeed moist with her tears. She hadn't even realized she'd been crying. "I suppose they are."

His hazel eyes searched her face. "Might I hope they are tears of happiness?"

A giggle bubbled up inside of her. "You may," she replied. "I have never been so happy in all my life."

"Then you know exactly how I feel," he said, just before he captured her lips again and kissed her completely senseless.

When he pulled away, he stared down at her, his eyes so full of love and tenderness, Hannah thought she might cry all over again. He stroked a finger down her cheek.

"I'm afraid I must go," he whispered.

Hannah didn't want him to, but she knew he'd be back. She knew she'd see him again, perhaps every day for the rest of her life, if she dared hope such a thing.

She nodded. "I understand."

"I will be back in the morning."

"I shall count the hours." Such a silly thing to say, and yet, she knew it was completely true.

His lips spread into a smile and then he bent down to give her one last swift kiss before leaving her room.

~*~

Graham could hardly believe what was happening. He'd kissed her, and she'd kissed him back. It was like a dream —a dream he'd never imagined could come true. But here they were, their feelings out in the open, sealed with a kiss. It was all Graham could do not to skip to his club that afternoon.

Plato's Assembly was a club comprised of men of intellect, and they met at a small coffee house in Spitalfields. Graham maintained a brisk walk on his way there, attempting to keep warm amidst the suddenly cooler weather. The sun had gone behind the clouds and rain threatened to pour down on him as gusts of wind tried to steal his hat away. But the one thing the wind couldn't steal from him was this buoyant mood.

He arrived at the coffee house and went directly to the back room where many of his friends and colleagues already sat about, sipping the strong Jamaican coffee that the establishment provided. All the way from the Blue Mountains, apparently. Good for one's rigor and fitness. Graham couldn't disagree—he always felt quite a bit livelier after a cup or two.

"Alcott!" His friend and scientist, Albert Baumgarten, waved at him from a nearby table at which sat Harry Cantor, another doctor, and Phillip Graves, a professor of Latin and Classic Literature at Oxford.

Graham gladly pulled up a chair to join them and promptly received a cup of coffee from the proprietor.

"Gentlemen," he said and then took a sip of coffee in hopes of concealing the smile he couldn't seem to wipe from his face.

Unfortunately, the men before him were quite astute, and his idiotic grin did not go unnoticed.

"What is this, my friend?" Cantor was the first to speak up. "If I didn't know better, I'd say you've had yourself a bit of fun lately."

Graves laughed. "But you *do* know better," he said, and then they all laughed, even Graham. He wasn't typically known for having fun—unless one counted endless hours of reading medical journals fun. Which he did.

"No, no," he said, holding up his hands as if in surrender, "Cantor is right. I have been having a bit of fun."

How to Care for a Lady

"With a bit o' muslin?" Baumgarten asked, his eyes wide with surprise.

"Good God, man! What do you take me for? I'm a doctor—I've much more sense than to seek out a syphilitic woman."

"Rather harsh, don't you think?" Cantor asked.

"Not harsh, just true. I've cared for plenty of those women, and I don't judge them for their profession. I'm just not going to bed one, is all."

Cantor nodded. "Point taken."

"Well, then," Graves said, leaning forward in his chair and placing his elbows on the rough, wooden table. "Who is she?"

"Unfortunately, I'm not at liberty to say." Then he added, "Not yet at least."

"Ah." Baumgarten relaxed against the back of his chair. "A patient, then."

"I never said anything of the sort. Just that I'm not at liberty to talk about it yet."

"We all know you're caring for the Widow Beeston," Cantor said, lowering his voice. "I would hesitate to engage in any—"

"It isn't her," Graham snapped. Damn his idiotic grin! He'd always prided himself on being able to mask his emotions —it came in handy when dealing with the ailing and downtrodden all the time. If he allowed his emotions to show, his patients would be in constant states of panic and fear, for many times the prognosis was heartbreaking.

"Fine," Cantor pressed. "But if it is, you should be warned."

An ominous silence fell over the table. Graham wanted to know what the hell his friend was talking about, but if he asked him to elaborate, would it implicate him in the affair? It took all his strength to keep silent, but thankfully, Cantor went on without provocation.

"It is rumored that Beeston isn't really dead."

A sick feeling stirred in Graham's belly. "What are you talking about?" he demanded.

"He might still be alive."

"Yes, I gathered that from your first statement," Graham bit back, growing exasperated with his colleague. "But why? And where are you getting your information?"

"A maid in the Hawthorne household heard it from a footman in the Hastings household who'd heard it from a stable boy in the Hart household who'd—"

"Dammit, man! Get to the point!" Graham slammed his fist on the table. "*What* did they hear?"

"That the Duke of Somerset may have paid off Beeston and sent him to America."

A coldness washed over Graham. He couldn't move. He couldn't speak. If Beeston was still alive, exiled or not, then Hannah was not a free woman. If Beeston came back to claim her—

No. He couldn't even fathom it. Surely, if this were true, the man wouldn't dare step foot on English soil again. Somerset would surely kill him for good this time.

Damn it all. He knew Somerset was a powerful man, but had he truly gotten the magistrate to fake a death certificate?

Graham shook his head. How did he know if there even *was* a death certificate? Perhaps everyone had simply taken him at his word.

"Excuse me, gentlemen," he said, standing abruptly and sending his heavy wooden chair backwards until it thudded to the floor. In a fluster, he righted it, and then swiftly quit the room. Perhaps his friends would suspect his smile *was* due to Lady Beeston now—how could they not draw that conclusion? But he was beyond caring at this point. He trusted them to keep the confidence. But his confidence in a certain duke had been swayed now, and duke or not, he owed him an explanation.

Or did he? Damn.

Graham stopped on the sidewalk outside the coffee house, vaguely aware of the noise and activity around him. His mind was whirling with the possible consequences of confronting the duke, even though every muscle in his body was aching to do so. But it was unlikely the man would take too well to being called out by a doctor. And then what would happen? More than likely he'd lose his post and never see Hannah again.

He closed his eyes and clutched his walking stick for support as people brushed past him. There was nothing for it. He was out of options. He couldn't confront the duke. He couldn't tell Hannah. He could only wait, and watch, and hope that what he'd just heard was only a rumor not grounded in any sort of truth.

FIFTEEN

Hannah could hardly contain her excitement. Today was to be her first outing since she'd been wounded. Now that Grace was feeling better thanks to Graham's ginger concoctions, Hannah would accompany her and her relations on a little shopping trip. Nothing terribly strenuous—just a visit to the modiste, where she and Grace could sit most of the time. She had a lofty dream that they might have a ready-to-wear gown for her that she could wear to Lady Wolverly's soiree in a few days' time. She knew Graham held her in high esteem no matter what she looked like—he'd seen her at her very worst, after all, and had still somehow fallen in love with her—but she still wanted to surprise him by looking her absolute smartest for his sister's party.

"Are you ready?" Grace asked, poking her head around the door of Hannah's bedchamber.

Hannah turned slowly from the mirror and smoothed her skirts, noticing that the color was back in Grace's cheeks. One would hardly have known that just a few days ago she could barely get out of bed.

"How do I look?" Hannah asked. She wore a day gown of dark lavender trimmed with a floral chintz pattern. Her maid had braided her hair into a crown on top of her head, leaving a few tendrils to peek out from beneath her yellow bonnet, which she was currently tying around her neck.

Grace smiled sweetly at her. "Oh, Hannah, we thought you'd never walk again, and now look at you. You're as lovely as ever."

"Well, perhaps not as *ever*," Hannah deflected, "but I must say, I'm feeling quite in my prime, even if I do walk with a bit of a limp."

"One can hardly even notice," Grace gushed. "Besides, there are lots of people who walk with limps. Miss Macintosh, for one. She had some awful disease as a child and never fully recovered."

And the girl used it to her every advantage. She was quite pretty and she knew it, so she often played Damsel in Distress with the young men of the *ton* who were more than happy to take pity on her and dance their attentions upon her. Of course, there were others who weren't so kind, but Miss Macintosh didn't seem to notice them. Hopefully, Hannah would be oblivious to those who might mock her as well.

"While that is meant to be comforting, this affliction is not something I would wish on anyone."

"Oh, of course you wouldn't," Grace said. "You're far too good-hearted for that."

"I am only that which God made me."

"Well, God made you the nicest of all, then."

Hannah laughed. "You're awfully nice yourself, you know?"

Grace scoffed. "Hardly! But it is kind of you to say so. I do love you so, Hannah."

"And I you," Hannah replied, taking her sister-in-law by the arm. "Shall we go?"

She limped alongside Grace to the carriage, which conveyed them across town to Regent Street, where they were to meet the others. Hannah was somewhat acquainted with all the Wetherby women—of course, Lady Chloe lived right next door, so she knew her best. Lady Chloe's cousin, who also happened to be her sister-in-law, wouldn't be in attendance, as she lived in Scotland. But the Duchess of Hart would be there, along with her sister-in-law, the Marchioness of Eastleigh, and the marchioness' dear friend, the Viscountess Hastings. She sincerely hoped that would be everyone. Being her first outing in so long, she was a bit nervous about becoming overwhelmed by all the activity.

"You needn't be nervous," Grace said, as if reading her mind. Or perhaps simply noticing that Hannah was mangling her skirts with her fingers as they rumbled along.

Hannah stopped her fidgeting. "There are so many of them," she replied, not bothering to deny that she was nervous.

"And they're all aware of the ordeal you've been through," Grace said. "They've promised to be...subdued today."

"Oh, goodness." That didn't really make Hannah feel any better. She didn't want anyone to compromise who they were for her sake. "They don't have to do that for me."

"But they want to. For both our sakes' really."

"You seem to be right as rain now," Hannah pointed out. "Dr. Alcott must have some magical spell he puts into all his concoctions."

"Indeed," Grace agreed. "I'm still a bit tired, and occasionally I'm surprised by a wave of nausea, but heavens, I feel so much better than I did."

Hannah was about to respond when the carriage came to a halt. She peered out the window to see they had pulled up in front of the modiste's shop, and a moment later, the door flung open for them.

"Thank you, John," Grace said to the driver as a footman handed her to the ground. "We won't be but an hour or so."

John nodded. "I shan't be far, milady."

Hannah stood on the sidewalk and took a deep breath before following Grace into the shop. They were all there already, poised around the sitting area with glasses of champagne in their hands. Her Grace, the Duchess of Hart, was the first to greet them in a whirl of red silk.

"There you are!" she exclaimed, rushing to kiss them each on the cheek. "You dear things, we're so glad to have you join us today. And I insist you call me Katherine, all right? Now, come say hello to the others."

If this was *subdued,* Hannah shuddered to think what the duchess was like on a regular day.

While Grace went around the room, greeting the others, the duchess refreshed Hannah on who everyone was—Lady Eastleigh, a lovely brunette with a kind smile, and Lady Hastings, a voluptuous blonde with eyes the color of emeralds. And of course, Lady Chloe, whose red hair seemed even more fiery today—Hannah wondered briefly if they'd be able to find her amidst all the brightly colored autumn trees were she to stand amongst them.

With the introductions out of the way, Hannah accepted a glass of champagne and a seat on the settee between Grace and Lady Chloe. She took note of how she was feeling, being careful not to overwhelm herself, but thankfully, she felt quite wonderful. The ladies chatted around her, sharing stories of their children and husbands, discussing the cooling weather and the soirees they'd be attending in the coming days. It was no surprise to hear they'd all be at the Wolverly soiree, which was rather comforting to Hannah—the more familiar faces, the better.

The modiste began a parade of fabrics, over which they all *Ooh'd* and *Ah'd.* The duchess was partial to the shiny silks and satins, while Lady Eastleigh was drawn to more practical, muted tones. Lady Hastings barely said a word after declaring she was quite content with her wardrobe as it was, and Lady Chloe seemed to share the sentiment. Grace merely stared longingly, complaining every now and again that it would be some time before she had a gown commissioned.

"Nonsense," Katherine finally exclaimed. "Just because you are *enceinte* doesn't mean you're dead. You should certainly have some dresses made for your confinement."

Grace sighed. "You really think so?"

"At least something pretty for Christmas," Lady Chloe, who had been mostly silent, put in.

"Oh, I suppose you're right." Grace cheered a bit. "Madame Morisette," she called without even bothering to use the correct French pronunciation, "might I see what you have in a dark green fabric?" Then she turned to the others. "Green over red, don't you think?"

They all nodded in agreement. Green was a lovely color on Grace.

Once her sister-in-law had chosen the fabric and trim and consulted every last fashion plate in the shop, the hour was up and it was time to go. Only, Hannah had yet to ask about any ready-made dresses.

Before Grace began saying her goodbyes, Hannah stopped her and addressed the proprietress. "Perhaps before we go, you could show me some ready-made dresses, Madame Morisette?"

Grace stared at her, wide-eyed, while the others smiled on.

"You're buying a dress?"

Hannah stared back. "I would like to," she replied. "Hardly anything fits me anymore, and I thought it might be nice to have something new for the Wolverly soiree."

And so began another half hour of assessing and trying on what the modiste had in her shop. There was a gown of dark olive with yellow and beige flowers embroidered along the edges, a red silk gown, not unlike the one the duchess wore today, with tiny black beads for trim, and finally, a white gown with a filmy white overlay, dabbed with blue embroidered flowers and trimmed with ruffles. They were all exquisite in completely different ways, and every lady in attendance had an opinion on which one they preferred. But Hannah wasn't really conflicted at all. She knew which one she wanted, and so, without hesitation, she asked the modiste to wrap it up, while Grace instructed the assistant to charge it to the duke's account.

At last, it was time to make their departure. Hannah was starting to wilt a bit, and she could see Grace was in need of a nap herself. They said their goodbyes and went out to the sidewalk. The Somerset crest gleamed from the side of the coach across the street, and John immediately moved to bring it 'round for them.

Hannah smiled as she looked up and down the street. It was all so lively and exciting—she'd missed this, being part of society, the hustle and bustle and—

"What is it?" Grace asked, and only then did Hannah realize her gasp had been audible.

But now she was frozen in fear, her heart racing, her lungs struggling to take in air.

"Hannah," Grace persisted. "What is it? What is the matter?"

Hannah blinked as she followed the figure with her eyes. A man with the same stature as her late husband. The same balding head. The same belabored stride, a result of too much wine and meat.

Grace must have spotted him too, for she grabbed Hannah's hand, now cold with fear. "It can't be," she whispered.

And then the man turned, sending relief rushing through Hannah's body. "Dear God," she muttered. "I do think my eyes are playing tricks on me."

"It wasn't just you," Grace said. "The resemblance was uncanny—until he showed his face, of course. Heavens, my heart can't take much of that."

"Mine either." Hannah pulled her sister-in-law by the hand toward the carriage. "Come. We both need a rest."

SIXTEEN

Ever since Graham had made the decision not to confront the duke about the allegedly deceased baron, he'd struggled to put it from his mind completely. It wasn't easy. It plagued him at all hours of the day, and even worse, at night. The lack of sleep was starting to show in the bags beneath his eyes, and he'd noticed his hand was a bit less steady in recent days. But on the day of his sister's soiree, he vowed to not think about Somerset or Beeston or anything that might ruin what was to come that evening.

He'd seen to Hannah that morning, and stolen a few kisses in the process, and after checking in on the duchess, who had very little use for him anymore, he went on his merry way to go and pick up the gift he'd commissioned for the baroness. The walking stick was even more beautiful than he'd imagined it would be. The sleek mahogany wood, the golden handle swirled with flowers and delicate birds—he prayed Hannah would love it.

He arrived at his sister's home earlier than he needed to. The guests wouldn't start arriving for another half hour at least, but he wanted to make certain she didn't need his assistance with anything. And furthermore, he was rather restless in anticipation of the announcement he and Hannah were going to make later on. In spite of the dark cloud of Beeston looming over him, it was the happiest day of his life. The day he would get to announce to the world that he loved Lady Beeston, and he wanted to take her for his wife.

"Graham!" Daphne said, spotting him from across the empty ballroom. "You're early."

They met in the middle of the room, and she stood on tiptoe to kiss him on the cheek. "Yes, well, I wanted to make certain you didn't need my assistance before the party started."

"No, no, all is taken care of. Except..." She peered around him toward the doorway. Graham turned to see his little niece and nephew peeking around the corner, full of giggles. "Wolf was supposed to be helping nanny tuck them into bed."

"Don't you dare go in there!" came Wolf's voice from somewhere outside the ballroom. Of course, the children took it as a challenge and ran headlong into the ballroom, Marcus barreling into his mother and Daisy making a beeline for Graham.

Graham scooped up his little niece, who was already clad in a soft, white nightgown, and kissed her on the cheek. "I think your father isn't too happy with you, my flower."

Daisy only giggled as Wolf stalked into the ballroom, their frazzled nanny trailing along behind.

"Goodness, darling, have you no control over your own children?" Daphne said.

"Have you?" Wolf bit back.

"Touché." Daphne turned to the nanny. "*I* will help you put them to bed, Nanny."

Graham couldn't let his sister do that when she was minutes away from receiving guests for a party. "I'll go," he volunteered.

"Oh, Graham, don't be silly." She moved to go, but Graham stopped her.

"Don't *you* be silly. We will be fine, but you absolutely must be present when your guests start to arrive."

Daphne stared at him, clearly conflicted. She wanted to do everything for everyone all the time. But finally, she heaved a breath, and conceded. "Fine. Thank you."

"My pleasure."

With Daisy still in his arms, her head now resting upon his shoulder, Graham followed Nanny and Marcus upstairs to the nursery. By the time they arrived at the door, Daisy was sound asleep and Marcus was yawning and rubbing his eyes. It didn't take any time at all to get them tucked into bed, and then Graham bid Nanny goodnight before returning to the ballroom.

The first of the guests had arrived—Wolf's good friend, Sidney Garrick and his wife, Matilda, along with her sister, Lila and her husband, Lord Quentin Post. There was no sign cf Hannah yet, which made him a bit nervous, but he shoved his concern to the back of his mind and attempted to make conversation with the other guests while he waited.

Of course, he couldn't concentrate on anything anyone was saying. His eyes kept darting to the doorway, looking for her. Guest after guest poured in, and Graham thought to scold his sister for inviting so many people. It was supposed to be a small, somewhat private affair, being Hannah's first time reemerging into society. But there was nothing for it now—he couldn't turn away his sister's guests.

Graham was just about to seek out a glass of Scotch to calm his nerves, when he caught a glimpse of the Duchess of Somerset. His heart set to racing, and his palms grew sweaty as he peered left and then right, his gaze finally finding her.

"Dear God," he breathed. She was exquisite. And bold. For a woman who had spent many years being repressed by an ogre of a man, who had barely been able to lift her head off her pillow a couple months ago, it was hard to believe it was she standing there in a gown of scarlet. Deep, sensual scarlet. God, how he wanted to tear it from her body and kiss every last inch of her. He knew her so intimately as her doctor, but this was different. In no way were his thoughts in the vein of professionalism.

She turned and caught his eye, forcing him to catch his breath. Then she smiled sweetly and batted her eyelashes in the most innocent of ways, it was hard to imagine she was an experienced widow of thirty years.

Graham made his way through the crowd, nudging people aside when he had to, until he stood before her. They both stood still for a long moment, taking each other in, until finally, he murmured, "I have something for you."

Her eyes grew round. It wasn't terribly smooth in the way of a greeting, but he wanted her to have the new walking stick this evening. He offered his arm, and she took it, before he led her slowly out of the ballroom and down the corridor to the library, where he'd left the package.

"You didn't have to get me a gift," she said, as they entered the room, lit only by the fire and a few oil lamps strategically placed near the sitting areas.

"But I wanted to," he defended. "Now, hurry before anyone notices we're gone."

Hannah plucked the ribbon and it fell to either side of the long box, and then she lifted to the top to reveal the walking stick. It shone brightly in the firelight, accentuating the detail on the handle and the shiny, carved wood.

Hannah gasped. "Oh, Graham," she whispered. "It's... it's..."

Her face twisted as she stared at the gift, and tears shimmered in her eyes. She placed a hand over her heart, as if to help her catch a breath.

"Do you like it?" he asked quietly.

"Oh, Graham!" she said again, and then threw herself into his arms, crying against his shoulder.

"It's exquisite," she sniffled as she pulled away a moment later to look up at him. Her cheeks were stained with her tears but she wore a smile. "I shall be honored to walk with it tonight."

Graham's heart felt so full, he thought it might explode. She was everything to him, and he would find ways to make her cry tears of joy like this for the rest of his life.

He cupped her face in his hands and brushed away the tears with his thumbs, just before he leaned down to kiss her. Her lips were both sweet and salty, and he couldn't get enough. He wanted more, but that would have to come later. Tonight, they had an announcement to make, and he couldn't wait another moment.

He pulled the walking stick from the box and handed it to her. "My lady," he said. She took it from him and then he offered his other arm to her.

111

Together, they walked back to the ballroom, which had turned into quite a crush. Perhaps not quite as crowded as a springtime ball, but still a bit stifling for Graham's taste.

"There you both are!" Her Grace rushed toward them before they could get very far. "Oh, goodness, what an exquisite walking stick, Hannah!"

"A gift from Dr. Alcott," she said, pride in her voice, which made Graham smile.

But seeing as they'd not made their announcement yet, this came as quite a shock to the duchess. Her eyes and lips rounded in surprise as she turned her attention to him. "A rather expensive gift for a doctor to give to a patient."

"Actually," Hannah said, pulling Her Grace's attention back to her. "We've an announcement to make this evening. I suspect it won't seem so strange once you hear it."

The young duchess looked as if she might implode if someone didn't tell her the secret then and there. "An announcement?" she cried. "Is there…are you…oh, my!"

Hannah stepped forward and took her sister-in-law by the hand. "Grace, you must calm down," she whispered. "I know it is probably a bit of a shock, but, well…" She glanced back at Graham. "It was inevitable."

Silence fell over them as the duchess tried to grasp the situation, but at last, her face melted into something akin to happiness, and she pulled Hannah into her embrace.

"Oh, Hannah, I couldn't be happier for you! What wonderful news this is."

"You really think so?"

"I do! I do," she said, pulling away. "Dr. Alcott, what a blessing you have been to our family, and now this… Oh, I cannot express my joy adequately!"

"What the devil is going on over here?" Somerset approached their party, his face in a scowl, his dark curls shaking with every pounding step he took.

"Oh, Evan, wait until you hear!" the duchess said, grabbing onto her husband's arm. She was about to open her mouth to share the secret, but Hannah stopped her with a wave of her hand and a pointed look.

"Evan," she said carefully, "Grace has just found out that...well, that...that is to say, Dr. Alcott—"

"They're getting married!" Clearly the duchess couldn't take the suspense.

The duke's eyes rounded, much as his wife's had done moments earlier, and his piercing blue gaze landed on Graham. Graham's stomach did a flip, nervous all of a sudden about what the man might say about his sister marrying a doctor. And so soon after her husband's death. Damn, he'd not really thought all of this through, he'd been so enamored of Hannah. So deeply in love with her that he'd not considered all the scenarios. Except the one that possibly had Beeston still alive and well and coming back to claim his wife.

There was a long, uncomfortable pause before Somerset finally said, "A word, Dr. Alcott," and then stalked out of the ballroom.

"Oh, dear," Hannah whispered, turning her lovely brown eyes up to him. "I suppose we should have expected this."

"Don't worry," Her Grace put in. "He just needs a moment to get used to it. Go on, Doctor. It will all be fine."

Graham looked back to Hannah, and when she gave him a nod, he made his exit. Somerset awaited him in the corridor, and turned on his heel when he caught sight of Graham. Graham followed him back to the library and took a seat at the duke's suggestion. The duke, however, did not sit. He merely paced back and forth in front of him, his brow furrowed in deep thought. Was Graham supposed to speak first?

"I know this must be quite a shock," Graham started to say, but the duke held up his hand to silence him.

Then he stopped his pacing and looked directly at Graham, his hands clasped as if in prayer. "You cannot marry my sister," he said, and Graham's stomach plummeted.

"I understand you do not approve," Graham said. "But your sister is thirty years old, and a widow. She should be able to marry whomever she wishes."

"Under different circumstances, I would heartily agree with you."

That sick feeling started to wash over Graham again. That one he'd gotten that night at Plato's Assembly when he'd heard the rumor about Beeston. "What circumstances," he said slowly, "are we under, then?"

The man took a deep breath and closed his eyes, sinking into the chair just behind him. "Beeston is not dead."

SEVENTEEN

Dammit. The rumors were correct. But that didn't make him feel any better. On the contrary, it made him feel terrified. Beeston was out there, and if he so chose, he could come back and claim his wife. There were plenty of people who would try to stop him, but short of killing the man and facing death themselves, they had very little power.

He stared at the man before him—a man with more power than a thousand regular men combined. But even he had refrained from killing Beeston, much as he'd apparently wanted to.

"I had heard rumors to that end," Graham admitted. "But I had fervently hoped they weren't true."

Somerset leaned forward and put his face in his hands, clearly troubled. "He's supposed to be in America."

"What makes you believe otherwise?"

The duke took a deep breath. "Someone from my club claims to have seen him."

"Where? When?"

Somerset shook his head. "I didn't ask, fool that I am. I was so terrified if I asked too many questions, someone would find out what I'd done, and then…"

"Do you think anyone would fault you for it?"

"No." He shook his head. "No one except Hannah."

"Ah." Graham understood. He'd not wanted to upset her further. He'd wanted her to go on with her life in peace, not looking over her shoulder every moment. But that didn't make her any safer from the reprobate.

"I didn't expect her to want to marry again so soon. Hell, we thought she'd never get out of bed again, let alone be at a ball about to announce her engagement less than six months later."

"I think we're all a bit surprised," Graham put in. "No one more than me."

Somerset leveled him with his ice blue eyes. "Do you love her?"

"More than anything."

The duke nodded and looked away. "I do wish we could celebrate with a cigar and brandy, but I'm afraid I must cut my own time here short. I must find Beeston before he finds Hannah."

"Where do you plan to start?"

"I've no idea." Somerset shook his head. "But I'll pay a visit to the club and enlist some of my friends to help."

"I want to help too."

"No." Somerset held up a hand. "You stay with Hannah. Don't let her out of your sight unless she is safely ensconced in my home."

Graham was torn. He wanted to watch over Hannah, of course, but he hated that he wouldn't be able to help in the search for Beeston.

"There's only one reason Beeston would have returned to London," Somerset went on. "He sees Hannah as his possession."

"Then why did he leave in the first place?" Graham wondered.

"The money, most likely. Maybe a bit of shame, but that's hard to imagine with Beeston. The man is entirely self-serving. And calculating. Make no mistake—this was all planned. Play along with the duke's plans, and then swoop in when they least expect it to stake his claim."

"Sounds like a wonderful man," Graham said, his tone dripping with sarcasm.

The duke shook his head. "You've no idea." Then he stood, and Graham followed suit. "Now, get back to the ballroom and take care of my sister. Go on with your announcement as planned. And whatever you do, don't tell Hannah about any of this."

Graham nodded. He was in perfect agreement. "What do I say to Her Grace?"

Somerset gritted his teeth. "Damn. I'll never hear the end of it if I leave." He paused for a long moment. "There's nothing for it, though. Tell her I left on important business that I will tell her about tonight, at home."

"God speed, Somerset."

The duke rushed from the room and Graham followed at a slightly slower pace. When he arrived back at the ballroom, he stood in the doorway, looking for Hannah's head of shiny chestnut hair, but it proved rather difficult in the crush. At long last, he spotted the duchess and figured Hannah couldn't be too far off from her sister-in-law. He pushed through the crowd again, his eyes still scanning the ballroom as he did so, until he reached Her Grace.

"Dr. Alcott!" she said. "Have you seen my husband?"

"Actually, I have," he replied. "If I may have a quick word."

The duchess batted her long lashes. "Oh, of course." And then she excused herself from her present company to follow Graham to the alcove a few paces away. "What is it?"

"Somerset had to leave."

Fire immediately emblazoned her green eyes. "The devil he did," she seethed through clenched teeth. "Where has he gone?" She looked as if she was ready to go after him and drag him back by the ear.

"Believe me when I say," Graham began, his tone grave, "that he is on extremely important business, which he will explain to you in greater detail later. However, it is imperative that we find Hannah and not let her out of our sight the rest of the evening."

Her Grace's brows creased into a V. "Why? What is going on?"

"You will have to wait for Somerset to tell you that," he replied. "But Your Grace, where is Hannah?"

"She's..." The duchess lifted her hand and looked toward the balcony. "Getting some air."

~*~

"Hannah! Hannah!"

Hannah pushed herself off the wall where she'd been resting and staring out at the moonlight gardens. Goodness, what were Graham and Grace going on about? They strode about the balcony, calling her name so frantically, Hannah was starting to worry herself.

"I'm here!" she finally called, drawing their attention to her, and they both visibly deflated. "What in the world is the matter with you two?"

The pair approached, and Graham rushed to her, grabbing her firmly by her upper arms. "Are you all right?"

Hannah laughed. "Of course I'm all right. What is going on?"

Graham cleared his throat and gave a little laugh of his own as he looked to Grace. She tittered nervously. Something was most definitely going on.

"It's um..." Graham began, but trailed off.

"Time to make your announcement, of course!" Grace finished, seeming rather proud of herself. The two of them were acting strangely, and Hannah debated whether or not she should press the issue.

"Yes, our announcement. My sister..." He gestured toward the ballroom. "She's inside."

Hannah looked back and forth from Graham to Grace, and decided, in the end, to let it go. Whatever they were up to, they weren't going to be forthcoming about it, clearly. "Well, we shouldn't leave everyone waiting, then, should we?"

"Indeed we should not," Graham said, and then proffered his arm for her.

Hannah took it, and with Grace at their heels, they walked back into the ballroom. Well, *they* walked, Hannah limped. As they entered the space, packed with people, butterflies began to beat about in her stomach. Goodness, were

HOW TO CARE FOR A LADY

they really going to announce it here? In front of all these people? Did these people even *care*? She'd thought it was to be a small gathering of close friends—but Hannah barely recognized any of the faces here.

"Are you all right?" Graham asked, and only then did Hannah realize she'd come to a stop just inside the doors.

"Perhaps we should do this another time," she suggested.

Graham rounded on her, so they were face to face. "Are you not feeling well?"

She clutched his hands and stared up at him, in awe of the calming effect he seemed to have over her. "Just a bit nervous is all."

"I imagine that's completely normal," he replied. "Though I can't speak from experience."

"Come, you two!" Grace shouted from ahead, having just realized she was alone on her trek across the ballroom.

"I don't think I have much of a choice now anyway, do I?"

Graham laughed, and the sound made her heart skip a beat. "Probably not."

They caught up to Grace and all together, walked to where Graham's sister stood beside her husband. They were whispering to one another, and Daphne lowered her fan to let out a laugh, just before the group approached.

"Ah! My dearest brother," she said, going up on tip-toe to kiss him on the cheek.

Graham looked to Lord Wolverly. "How much champagne has she had tonight?"

"Oh, hush!" Lady Wolverly swatted at Graham with her fan. "I've barely had any. I'm just giddy over how wonderfully everything is going tonight. It really couldn't be more perfect."

"Well, I do believe your brother and my sister-in-law are ready to make their announcement," Grace put in.

"Oh, of course! Look! The quartet is just standing for a break—the timing couldn't be more perfect. Darling, you will get everyone's attention?"

Hannah suddenly felt as if she might toss up her accounts. Goodness, she was nervous. And yet, she knew, without any doubt, that this was right. It was what she'd always wanted—what she wanted for her future. He was everything to her, and the smile he cast her told her he felt the same way.

Graham took her hand and led her toward the raised dais, upon which the quartet had just finished their second set for the evening. At the same time, Lord Wolverly clanked a spoon to his glass, and slowly, the ballroom descended into silence.

Daphne took her place beside them. "Ladies and Gentlemen, I must first extend my thanks to all of you for joining us tonight, and I do hope everyone is enjoying themselves to the fullest. I am thrilled to announce that my brother, Dr. Graham Alcott, has asked the esteemed Lady Beeston to be his bride, and she has said yes! I know you will all join Lord Wolverly and I in congratulating the happy couple!" Grace lifted her glass of champagne toward them. "To you!"

Shouts of "Here, here!" and "Many felicitations!" rang out through the ballroom, though Hannah was certain she'd heard a few gasps here and there as well. But it was out there now, and there was nothing anyone could do or say that would change her mind about marrying this wonderful man.

EIGHTEEN

"Are you happy?"

"Don't I *look* happy?" Hannah's cheeks hurt from smiling so much, for she was, indeed, very happy. The happiest she'd ever been, to be truthful. When she thought of how she'd gone from her mother's home—the cold, unfeeling, strict home that it had been—into Beeston's home, which offered even less in the way of comfort, it was hard to believe she'd landed here, with Dr. Graham Alcott. A kind and generous man, who cared for her like no one ever had.

He bent down and captured her lips, further assuring her that she'd made the right decision in accepting his proposal of marriage. He was firm and coaxing, and she opened easily, gladly for him, allowing him access not just to her mouth, but to her soul.

"If you would be so kind as to tear yourselves apart."

The sharp voice from the doorway sent Graham and Hannah stumbling away from one another. Hannah had to tighten her grip on her walking stick to keep from crashing to the ground.

"Mother," she said, her breathing belabored. "You ought to have announced yourself."

"Oh, *ought* I?" Mother sauntered into the dimly lit room, her black bombazine swishing loudly, the high, stiff collar making her look like some dark Elizabethan queen who had a penchant for chopping off heads. "As it turns out, this is a public area, where anyone might be permitted to go. I know you are engaged, but you wouldn't want anyone to think you're fast, would you? Of course," she looked Hannah up and down with a shrewd eye, "such speculations might have already been drawn from your choice of attire."

It was remarkable how this woman still had the power to make her feel small and ashamed, even after all she'd been through. "Clearly, you've something to say, Mother."

Her mother sucked in a sharp breath through her pointed nose and turned her attention to Graham. "I've only to say, welcome to the family, Dr. Alcott."

Well, that was unexpected.

Graham dipped his head. "Thank you, Your Grace. I must admit, we weren't certain how you would feel about our union."

"Which would explain why I found out with the rest of the masses, when it was too late to have a say in the matter." She turned a pointed look on Hannah.

"It wouldn't have mattered, Mother," she said, puffing up her chest in hopes of feeling slightly braver. "I'm a widow, not a debutante. The choice is mine and mine alone."

"And you're certain you wish to marry a doctor?"

"I am."

"And lose your title?"

"Nothing will make me happier than losing Beeston's name."

A hint of a smile turned the corners of Mother's lips up, but she did her best to hide it by casting her glance downward. "Well, then that is that, isn't it? Grace and I will be leaving soon. She's looking a bit peaked."

Hannah was feeling a bit tired herself. She glanced to Graham, and he seemed to read her thoughts. "Go with them," he said. "I much prefer to retire at a reasonable hour, myself."

"Very good," Mother said. "Come and find us when you are done here."

"Yes, Mother."

They stood in silence as the dowager swished her way out of the room, purposefully leaving the door open. Once she was out of earshot, Hannah turned to Graham, the breath whooshing out of her.

HOW TO CARE FOR A LADY

"My heart is pounding," she said, clutching her hand to her breast.

"*Your* heart?" Graham replied. "That woman is quite terrifying."

"I'm well aware." Hannah moved closer to him. "I know I didn't need her approval, but it makes things easier to actually have it."

"Agreed. Otherwise, I might have had to steal you off to Gretna."

She smiled up at him, losing herself in his gray-green eyes. "I would have gladly gone."

And then he lowered his head to hers and claimed her lips again. He was so tender it made her heart ache. All she'd ever wanted and longed for was wrapped up in this brilliant man.

At last he pulled away, a smile gracing his lips. A smile just for her. "Now, go," he said. "Lest someone think you're fast."

Hannah couldn't help but giggle. "Oh, we wouldn't want that."

Then he pulled her close for one last kiss. "Goodnight, my love."

"Goodnight."

~*~

As much as Graham wanted to spend every waking moment with Hannah, he was desperate to track down Beeston and...

And what? Kill him with his bare hands and sit in Newgate the rest of his life? Or worse, face the gallows? Deliver him to the magistrate and demand justice be served? Justice for what? For being a boorish husband? If that were the criteria for being locked up, most of England's men would be there with him.

Dammit. Somerset was right. Graham needed to look after Hannah and let him deal with Beeston. The thought made him ill. He wanted to *do* something, not just sit about waiting to hear the fate of the degenerate. But devil take it, there was nothing for it. He would look after Hannah as planned. Make certain she was safe when her family wasn't about.

But what was he to do now? The thought of going home and reading documents about diseases of the liver held very little interest to him tonight. His mind would never be able to focus. Not after simultaneously becoming engaged and learning his fiancée's husband was still bloody alive.

He banged his fist on the desk.

"I do wonder what the desk ever did to you?" came a slow, familiar drawl from the doorway.

Graham turned to find Sidney Garrick leaning against the threshold, his blond hair shining in the candlelight, his grin sly and mischievous, as it had always been. Wolf's oldest friend, he was also his opposite in every way. Where Wolf was mature, Sidney was boyish. Where Wolf was responsible, Sidney was reckless. And yet, they'd been friends since their earliest days at Eton.

Graham sometimes wished he had such a friend, but he'd always kept to himself, and kept most people at arms' length. Perhaps the fact that he dealt with people's mortality so often made him less inclined to form intimate relationships.

Of course, he'd had little choice with Hannah. The thought of losing her terrified him half to death. But the thought of never loving her was even worse.

"Garrick," he said at long last. "I saw you on the dance floor earlier. Quite impressive, you and your bride."

Arms folded across his chest, he sauntered into the library. "She forces me to practice the waltz at least four times a week."

"Is that so?" Graham replied, unable to picture Sidney Garrick being forced to do anything.

"I'm afraid it is." He plopped down onto one of the chairs and put his feet up on the coffee table. Graham was certain Daphne would scold him for such a thing, but Graham wasn't interested in acting as nursemaid to Garrick. "But don't worry...she always rewards me for it."

Of course, Garrick would turn the conversation to something lewd. "I shall have to take your word for it."

"What are you doing hiding out in here, anyway? Shouldn't you be dancing attention on your new fiancée?"

"She's going home with her mother and sister-in-law. I was just trying to plan what I was going to do with myself."

"Well, don't look at me. Tilly will have me dancing until the wee hours and then...well, you know." He winked at Graham.

"You enjoy, my friend. I think I shall see myself home, after all."

"Before you go..."

Graham stopped on his way to the door and turned around to face Garrick, who had removed his feet from the table and now sat forward, his elbows on his knees.

"There are rumors."

Damn. It seemed everyone knew about the bloody rumors. "Beeston?"

Garrick nodded. "I haven't seen him, but Quent and Bradenham have. In broad daylight. It's as if he *wants* the rumors to circulate."

"He's a rather sick man, from what little I've heard. It is impossible to understand the mind of a mad person. They do odd things, and for no apparent reason."

"Just be careful," Garrick said, and it suddenly became clear why he and Wolf had remained friends all these years. He was a good man with a genuine heart, no matter how childish he seemed at times. This was what it meant to have a true friend.

"Thank you," Graham said, and he meant it. "You will send word if you see him?"

"Immediately."

Graham nodded, and with that, set off for home.

NINETEEN

Hannah couldn't decide if it was unfortunate that she'd forgotten her shawl in the library, or fortuitous. For if she hadn't gone back to retrieve it, she never would have learned that Beeston was still alive.

She'd run from the room once she'd heard all she could stomach, making a beeline straight for the ladies retiring room. It was blessedly empty, and she was able to toss up her accounts in peace. Well, as much peace as her churning mind and stomach would allow.

Dear God. How could this be? He was dead. Mother and Evan, they'd told her so. They'd come to her room, heads hung, a note in Beeston's own hand, saying goodbye forever. She'd been conflicted at the time—riddled with both guilt and joy simultaneously. He was gone, but was it her fault? For months she'd toiled over that question. It had kept her up at night—another reason for the heavy doses of laudanum.

Oh, how she wished for some now. She just wanted to go to sleep and forget any of this had ever happened.

Tears rushed down her cheeks, and she stifled her sobs as best she could, but fear and anger and sheer sadness engulfed her. How would she get through this? How would she get past Beeston? How would she ever forgive her brother and mother for deceiving her in this way?

And Graham. He knew, and yet he'd not come rushing to tell her. He ought to have. She needed to know he was out there, that he could strike at any moment.

The thought of going back to Beeston made her wretch all over again. If he found her, and claimed her, there was very little anyone could do. She was his wife, so long as he was living. And no doubt he was angry now, after being forced to relinquish her. God help them all if he heard about her engagement.

Oh, God. The engagement. The announcement. She had to stop it from being printed in the papers tomorrow. But what good would that do now that so much of the *ton* knew firsthand that they were getting married? The news would fly through the *ton* tomorrow, whether in the papers or not.

Goodness, it was all scandalous enough, wasn't it? The barely widowed baroness finds love with the doctor who nursed her back to health after her boorish husband shot at her. What a tale she had weaved. It would be a fascinating one for generations to come, if only she were able to bear children.

Only then did the thought occur to her that Graham might want children. Heavens. What if he wanted them? She hadn't been terribly forthcoming with him about her situation. Would he still want her if he knew she was barren?

The tears wouldn't stop, not now. Not when she'd made such a mess of her life. It had been pathetic before, but now that she'd tasted a bit of true love, a hint of what true happiness was, it would be positively unbearable.

Voices out in the corridor drew her attention, and she swiped at the tears that moistened her cheeks. Blast it all, she had to pull herself together. What if someone saw her like this? She didn't want anyone to think her tears had to do with Graham, but she also didn't want to admit she knew Beeston was alive. She would sound mad to those who thought him dead. She sounded mad to her own self. It was all madness, and the thoughts threatened to send the tears rushing again, but she choked them back. A skill she'd perfected over the years. How many times had she hidden her tears and heartache behind a smile? More times than she wanted to count, really. But the practice would come in handy tonight.

She approached the mirror and took several deep breaths as she stared at her reflection, willing the redness out of her eyes. "You will get through this," she said to her reflection, thinking of that day many months ago when she'd stared at herself, and noted the sadness in her eyes. But lately, the sadness had been absent, replaced with the sparkle of youth she'd once had, long ago, before Beeston. Before she'd known what kind of man Beeston was, what kind of cruelty he was capable of.

Graham. He was not like Beeston at all. He was the kind of man Beeston most likely poked fun at. Quiet, kind, a man who revered women rather than viewing them as some thing he could use when it was convenient for him and toss them away a moment later. He was more man than Beeston would ever be.

By the time Grace barged through the door of the retiring room, clutching her chest and sighing with relief as she collapsed onto a tufted stool, Hannah's eyes were dry and white again, her resolve quite set.

"Grace!" she said, whirling to look at her sister-in-law properly rather than through the mirror. "Are you all right?"

"Fine," Grace puffed. "I just...I didn't...that is..."

Hannah smiled at her. Did she know about Beeston? Had she been worried that Hannah had been abducted by the blackguard? No, he wouldn't dare come here, would he? He would pounce when she least expected it. "Catch your breath," she said.

Grace took a moment to do just that and after a few moments, said, "I was looking for you."

"Goodness, I am sorry," Hannah said. "I didn't mean to worry anyone. I needed the, um..." She glanced to the partition, behind which sat a chamberpot.

"Of course," Grace replied, her color returning to normal. "I'm just glad, that is...your mother is ready to depart."

"As am I." Hannah grabbed her sister-in-law's hand and pulled her up to stand. She was fully prepared to pretend she knew nothing about Beeston, and to excuse her sister-in-law's odd behavior, but then an idea formed in her mind. An idea that would require...assistance. She could accomplish it on her own, of course, but it would take longer and be much more difficult. Not to mention, trying to hide it from her entire family whilst living beneath their roof. An ally would be most helpful. "Grace," she said, catching Grace's gaze.

"Mm-hm?" Poor girl looked like the cat that swallowed the canary, what with her wide eyes and pursed lips.

"I know," Hannah said simply.

It took only a moment for Grace to realize what she was talking about, and then she collapsed back to the stool once again. "Oh, thank goodness! You don't know what a burden it has been to carry that secret!"

Hannah cocked her head sideways. "How long have you known?"

"Since earlier this evening."

It was all Hannah could do not to fall off her own stool with laughter. Poor Grace, never able to hold onto secrets too long. "Well, you needn't carry it alone any longer. While I don't know all the details, I do know he's alive. One day soon, I will confront Evan on the matter. However, I need your help. I have a plan to bring Beeston to his knees, and I cannot do it alone."

TWENTY

When Graham arrived at the Somerset townhome the next morning, he was met with a grave looking Somerset. The man wore a frown even deeper than usual and immediately summoned Graham to his study. There was no denying the sick feeling in Graham's belly. Something was amiss—he only prayed Hannah was safe. Anything else could be dealt with, he was sure.

"Have a seat," Somerset said, gesturing to the empty leather chair and then making his way to the sideboard, where he poured two rather generous helpings of brandy. He handed one to Graham and then rounded the desk to sit on the other side. He took a drink; Graham followed suit.

Silence.

"Somerset, are you going to tell me why I'm here?" Graham asked, eager to get upstairs to Hannah.

"I think Hannah knows."

Graham nodded. He wasn't certain how to feel about that. What would it do to her? She was fragile enough as it was—news like this could...

"Why do you think that?" he asked, moving to the edge of his seat and setting his glass down on the desk.

"Grace found this—" The duke procured a small bottle. "—beside Hannah's bed."

Damn. She'd reverted to the blasted laudanum. There was no doubt now that she knew. Graham pushed back his chair and stood.

"Where are you going?"

"To reassure my bride-to-be that as long as I'm alive, no harm will come to her. She needn't resort to such measures just because that *man*—if one can even call him that—is still alive and in London."

"I don't know why she didn't come to me. Or you. *Anyone*! She must know we will protect her and do all we can to keep him away. No doubt, she is worried about your engagement, and what all of this means in terms of your marriage."

No doubt. "We will go on as if nothing has happened," Graham insisted. "The banns will be read, preparations made, and we will marry in six weeks' time."

"And what if Beeston does lay claim to her."

Then I shall kill him. A thought that frightened the devil out of Graham, and yet he'd lain awake last night plotting just how he might do it without getting caught. He couldn't tell that to the duke, though, so he simply shook his head, and said, "I don't know."

He stormed through the house and up the stairs until he stood at Hannah's door. Part of him was angry with her for picking up that damn bottle. After all they'd been through, all she'd overcome, and now she was going to send herself right back to bed, her body soaked in opiates, and pretend none of it ever happened? Sure, the news of Beeston was distressing, even to him—certainly it was catastrophic in her mind. But it didn't have to be. They would figure it out together, even if it meant running away to China or Australia or some far-off place where no one would care that her husband was still alive.

But to what lengths would Beeston go to claim his bride? Would they always have to look over their shoulders? Would they always wonder if he was nearby, watching, waiting for his moment?

Damn!

"Dr. Alcott?" The young duchess glided down the corridor toward him, her peach gown billowing around her legs.

"Your Grace," he said, offering her a bow. "How are you feeling today? I do hope last night's party wasn't too taxing for you."

"Not at all," Her Grace said, and then she drew in closer and lowered her voice. "Not for me, anyway."

Graham nodded. "Your brother has already enlightened me on the situation. But we mustn't fear a minor setback. I cured her of the addiction once, and I'm certain I can do it again."

"But can you promise her that Beeston won't come to claim her?"

No. He couldn't. And it was eating him up inside. "I will say what I have to in order to get her better."

"Please," she said, reaching out and squeezing his hand. "Do what you must."

She moved on and Graham faced the door again. His heart was heavy with sadness and frustration over the whole situation—he couldn't imagine how Hannah was feeling.

After a deep breath, he knocked three times in rapid succession and then pushed through the door. All the curtains were drawn closed, the only light a tiny sliver coming from the sun that sneaked through the edges of the drapes. The scene was almost identical to the one he'd come upon months and months earlier, when he'd first begun to care for Hannah. When she was weak and unable to care for herself. She'd come so far, he couldn't bear to see her reverted to this. It nearly broke his heart.

He approached the bed where she lay sleeping, the covers pulled tightly around her, a part of the fabric balled into her fist.

"Hannah," he whispered, kneeling down so that when she opened her eyes, she'd see his face. "Hannah, are you awake?"

She blinked her eyes open and it took a moment for her to realize who was there with her. Then her lower lip began to tremble and she closed her eyes again. "He's alive," she whispered.

HOW TO CARE FOR A LADY

Graham moved to sit on the bed and gathered her into his arms. "I know, my love," he murmured into her hair. "I know all about it."

He rocked her back and forth as she held onto him, quietly crying against his chest. "I took some laudanum last night."

A sigh escaped Graham. "Yes, I know about that too. Grace told me."

"I couldn't sleep."

"I don't imagine anyone could after hearing their husband had come back to life."

"What if he comes for me?"

Graham didn't know how to answer that. He knew what he wanted to do if that happened, but he'd do Hannah no good in Newgate. "I don't know," he said. "But I do know that I will do everything in my power to keep him from getting near you. Tell me...how do you feel about Australia?"

Hannah pulled back and stared at him, her tearful eyes shimmering in the dim room. "Australia?" she repeated with a bit of disdain in her tone.

"Or China?"

"China!"

"India?"

"Heavens, Graham," she said. "I don't want to leave England."

Damn. "Then we will find another way," he replied, at a loss for what that *other way* might be. "But you must promise me two things..."

She blinked at him.

"You must not take even another drop of laudanum."

She swallowed. "Fine."

"You must not leave this house without your brother or myself by your side."

She hesitated, but finally said, "Fine."

"We don't know what he has planned, Hannah," Graham went on, unsatisfied with her reluctant answer.

133

"Perhaps he plans to reclaim you. Perhaps he plans something worse."

Hannah pursed her lips together and nodded. Clearly, she'd considered that possibility—that perhaps he wanted to torture or even kill her. The thought made Graham absolutely sick to his stomach. If that bastard harmed even a single hair on her head, he'd have hell to pay.

"And I want you to know that this changes nothing," he went on. "The banns will be read, and we will be wed in six weeks."

"But what if—"

He placed a finger to her lips. "There is no room for 'what if.' This matter will be settled before then one way or the other, and you will be my bride."

Her lips spread into a grin beneath his finger, which he replaced with his lips. He promised her, with his kiss, that she had nothing to fear, that she was his, and no man—not even Beeston—would tear them asunder.

~*~

It was all Hannah could do to not pull Graham against her and beg him to have his way with her. How she wanted to feel his body pressed to hers, his hands roaming her bare skin. She ached for him all over. But she had work to do, so she would have to find a way to stave him off, much as it pained her.

She pulled away from the kiss and pretended to yawn. "I am still feeling the effects of the laudanum, my love," she said sleepily, burrowing back into the covers. "I fear I must rest some more."

He caressed her hair. Such a simple gesture that somehow had the power to make her feel so safe and adored. "Of course," he said. "You should sleep. You will feel back to yourself by tomorrow."

"I do hope so."

He leaned down and kissed her cheek. "I will see you then."

She nodded and closed her eyes, then waited. He walked slowly to the door, clearly taking care not to disturb her, now he thought she was asleep, then at long last, the latch clicked, and she was alone again.

Of course, she would have to wait a while longer before she could get up and prepare to leave. He might take time to speak with Mother or Evan before he left, and any one of them might come to check on her. But with any luck, he would urge them to leave her alone to sleep off the laudanum.

The laudanum she hadn't really taken.

Thank heavens for Grace. She was more than excited to play a part in Hannah's scheme, and right now she was compiling a very important list on her behalf. Once Hannah had the list in hand, she would set out on her mission, and Grace would have the arduous task of convincing the rest of the family to leave Hannah alone. Hannah, who wouldn't even be in the house, let alone lying in her bed feeling sorry for herself.

Satisfied that Graham was downstairs by now, Hannah rushed to the window, tucked into the corner of the widow seat, and pulled the curtain back just enough to see the street below.

It was all a bustle—mothers with their children, businessmen rushing about, aristocrats trying to avoid beggars —and there was Graham, his black bag in one hand, walking stick in the other. So tall and handsome, he stood out in the crowd, and Hannah smiled, knowing that soon enough, he would be hers. She just had to settle the little matter of Beeston first. Easier said than done, she was sure, but she had to try. She had to make certain he never did to another woman what he'd done to her.

Grace burst through the door a moment later, out of breath and flushed. But of course she wore a smile on her face. She absolutely lived for this sort of thing.

"Do you have the list?" Hannah asked, moving from the window toward her sister-in-law.

Grace procured a piece of paper from her bosom. "Here," she said. "Veronica Delaney."

"The actress?" Hannah confirmed.

Grace nodded. Hannah wasn't certain how she felt about this all of a sudden. Confronting her husband's paramours was going to be odd, to say the least. Perhaps a bit disturbing. Would they bear a resemblance to her? Or would they reflect a different preference of his altogether? Would she have to face her own shortcomings and wonder what it was he saw in them that he didn't see in her?

"You're trembling," Grace pointed out. "Perhaps you should reconsider—let Evan and Dr. Alcott handle this."

"No." The mere suggestion reminded Hannah why she was doing this. She couldn't let someone else fight her battles anymore. "I must do this. Is the carriage ready?"

"Leave out the servants' door and head to the mews. John will be waiting for you there with the unmarked carriage."

"And you've assured his discretion?"

"With a heavy coin purse, yes."

"Good." Hannah grabbed Grace's hands. "Thank you," she said. "I'll be back soon."

TWENTY-ONE

Hannah could only hope that this would get easier as time went on. As it was, her nerves were on edge and she hadn't stopped trembling the entire journey to the west end of town. A million thoughts whirled through her mind, making her belly turn over and over with each new one. What if Miss Delaney reacted badly to her? What if she turned her away? Or the most horrifying thought of all: what if Beeston was with her right now? Wouldn't that be just her luck?

But she couldn't think about that. She had to at least try, didn't she? Otherwise, she would regret not doing so every day of her life.

As the carriage came to a stop somewhere near Covent Garden, Hannah affixed the black fascinator to her hair and pulled the black lace veil over her face. With any luck, her widow's weeds would keep her from being recognized, as the clothing covered practically every inch of her and eclipsed her face almost entirely.

John opened the door and helped her down from the conveyance.

"Stay near," she instructed. "I won't be long." And then she looked down at the small piece of foolscap in her hand that instructed her on where to go.

It wasn't the worst part of town, but it wasn't the best either. It was far too close to Seven Dials for Hannah's comfort, but thankfully, it seemed Miss Delaney had a fairly nice set up in Covent Garden proper, if the outside of the building was any indication. No doubt a wealthy suitor had seen to her every need.

Hannah stared up at the townhome for a long moment before finally knocking on the door. Then she waited. And waited. And—

Nothing.

Disappointment flooded her, and she began to turn from the door, trying not to turn melancholy over the situation. There were many other women, much as she hated to admit that. It didn't mean her mission was over by any means. It just meant —

"Who are you?" came a voice from behind her.

Hannah whirled to find the door to the townhome cracked just enough to see part of the woman's face.

"My name is Hannah," she said, the words coming out far more steady than she felt. "Are you Miss Delaney?"

"What's your business?"

"I only want to talk to you—it won't take long, I swear. I just—" she glanced down the street, becoming nervous all of a sudden that someone might see her standing here, talking to the door. "It requires discretion. If I may come in."

There was a slight pause, and then the door eased open, allowing her entry into the foyer.

"Follow me," Miss Delaney said, leading her to a door just past the staircase.

They entered a small parlor that was well-appointed, but a bit dim, seeing as the only light came from a single window at the back of the townhouse. Hannah took a seat across from the woman, unable to stop herself from assessing her, head to toe.

She was blonde and quite beautiful by anyone's standards. She was of a similar height to Hannah, it seemed. Not short, not tall, simply average. But she was built quite a bit differently, with far more curves, to put it gently. If she wasn't careful, she'd spill right out the front of her gown. Given that, it was easy to see what Beeston saw in her.

"Who are you?" she asked, pulling Hannah's gaze from where it should not have been, back to her round, cherubic face.

"Hannah," she replied simply, at first. "Hannah Ludlum. Lady Beeston."

It wasn't until the last that Miss Delaney registered who she was. Her eyes grew round, and she began shaking her head frantically. "I don't want any trouble," she said, her cockney accent barely seeping through. "I swear, I didn't know he was married."

"Please," Hannah said, holding up a hand to stop her from blathering on. "I'm here as a friend."

That took the woman quite off guard. "A friend?"

Hannah nodded. "Indeed. You see, my husband was... well, not a good husband at all, as you might imagine. As a matter of fact, he shot me."

"Yes, I know," the woman replied. "That's the first I'd heard of you. From the papers. Then he came here, all distraught, going on about what he'd done and that he had to leave town."

Now it was Hannah's turn to be caught off guard. "You mean, the two of you were still...?" She couldn't say the words, so she simply waved her hand about, as if to indicate she was talking about intimate relations.

Miss Delaney nodded. "Not that I was the only one."

Hannah swallowed down the bile that rose to her throat. What a disgusting, odious man. To think she'd allowed him into her bed. Of course, she'd not had much of a choice, being his wife and all, but still, it made her stomach lurch to even think about it.

"No," Hannah muttered. "Of course not."

"If you've come to yell at me, I pray you get it over with."

"Oh." Hannah looked up at the woman. Funny to think she'd actually put fear into her. No one ever feared Hannah. "No, you misunderstand," she said. "I've come to ask for your help." She moved forward on her seat. "You see, Beeston took his own life—"

Miss Delaney gasped.

"Or so I thought," Hannah finished, and the woman relaxed in relief. "As it turns out, my brother only sent him away, to America. But he's come back, and I fear he plans to reclaim me."

"Reclaim you?"

Hannah nodded. "Of course he doesn't care for me. To him, I am but a mere possession. Something that rightfully belongs to him. And knowing him as I do, he will stop at nothing to get me back. If that happens, I will have little recourse. I am legally his wife, after all."

Miss Delaney just stared at her with her wide, blue eyes, waiting for Hannah to continue.

"Tell me," Hannah said. "Did you care for Beeston?"

That elicited a snort that was most certainly made of derision. "No one cared for Beeston but Beeston, my lady. But he paid for all this and kept food on my table."

"He...?" Hannah looked about. "Beeston paid for this?"

"Said he didn't want to keep having relations in my Seven Dials residence."

Hannah couldn't blame him there.

"So he set me up here."

"How have you afforded the rent since he left?"

"Paid it through the end of the year, he did," Miss Delaney said. "After that, I suppose I'll be out on the street."

Hannah needed a moment to think it all through, to grasp everything she'd just heard. She glanced about the room, realizing that Beeston had used his money—*their* money—to make certain this woman had a clean place to...to...

Oh, she couldn't even think it. But she also couldn't bear the thought of this poor woman being turned out on the street in the middle of winter.

"Of course we will figure something out for you," Hannah said, rendering Miss Delaney speechless. "You may have had relations with my husband, but you weren't the first. And I can't imagine what kind of situation would make you so desperate for money to sleep with such an odious man, so no, I do not lay the blame at your feet, Miss Delaney. You were a victim, as I imagine all his paramours were. As I feel I was.

HOW TO CARE FOR A LADY

Trapped by his charm at first, and then forced into what I feared would be a lifetime of loneliness and abuse from that man."

"You said you needed my help?"

"Indeed, I do." She reached into her reticule and procured the list Grace had made for her of all Beeston's known paramours. It was quite long—twenty-six women, to be exact—and there was no guarantee they'd all be as willing as Miss Delaney, but Hannah could hope.

She handed the list to Miss Delaney.

"What's this?"

"A list of his lovers," Hannah said, choking a bit on the last word. "I want to find all of them, so that together, we can make certain Beeston leaves town and never comes back."

Miss Delaney looked at the list, then back up at Hannah. "You want to trap him?"

"Better to trap him before he traps me." She paused. "Do you know any of them?"

"Some."

"Miss Delaney," Hannah said, reaching across the divide and taking the woman's hand. "Will you help me?"

The woman looked down at the list, then to Hannah's walking stick, and finally her gaze settled on Hannah. "Yes."

141

TWENTY-TWO

Graham knew he ought not to beat himself up over the situation—he was doing the best he could, after all—but he couldn't help it. Hannah was taking laudanum again, and her behavior was most troubling. Even worse, the duchess was defending and protecting her, insisting Hannah was a grown woman who could do as she pleased, and if laudanum helped her through this difficult time, Graham ought not to interfere.

It was ridiculous. He was her doctor first, fiancé second. He had more rights to tell her what to do than anyone else. And yet, in the face of the young duchess, he felt impotent. She was pushy and overbearing and so very loyal to her sister-in-law it was maddening.

"Are you going to sit there all day and watch her sleep?" came a voice from the doorway. Not the young duchess, thank God, but the dowager. He couldn't take much more of Her Grace today.

"That was my plan," he replied, turning back to Hannah's sleeping form. "Has she eaten at all since yesterday morning?"

The dowager took her place at the other side of the bed. "Not that I know of."

Damn. She would waste away to nothing again. He had to do something, but what? It clearly wasn't enough that he was combing the streets night and day, looking for Beeston. Or that they were to be married in five weeks' time. She'd fallen into despair and succumbed to the opiates again, and Graham felt completely helpless.

"Has Somerset had any luck tracking down Beeston?"

The dowager shook her head and sighed as she leaned back against the small, wooden chair. "I don't think so. Apparently, someone saw him near Spitalfields, entering what seemed to be an apartment. But whether or not it is his or some doxy's, no one knows."

"Perhaps I will go there today." He stared at his fiancé, his love. "I had hoped she would wake. I want to take her walking in the park, for ices at Gunters...to sit a spell on the verandah, at the very least, and talk about our future. Something. *Anything*."

"It isn't safe for her to be out and about anyway."

"She would be safe with me."

"Find Beeston, and all will be as it was before."

He could only hope. "You will alert me to any changes?"

The dowager nodded, and Graham stood. He bent over to place a kiss on Hannah's forehead and then left, praying the dowager was right.

~*~

The door clicked shut, but Hannah didn't trust that her mother had left with Graham. Oh, how painful that had been, to hear him speak of all the wonderful things they ought to be doing during their engagement. How she wanted to walk with him and eat ices with him, and she would. They had a lifetime for that. But for now, she had to make certain Beeston never dared to show his face in England ever again. And such a plan required the utmost discretion. Evan and Graham would never have allowed her to visit all the women she'd visited over the last week.

"Aren't you going to get up now?"

A gasp escaped her at the sound of her mother's voice and her heart sped to a dangerous pace. Still, she lay still. She'd gotten quite good at pretending to sleep lately.

"Hannah, do you think me daft? Get up. You owe me some explanations."

Hannah felt like a young girl again, cornered by her overbearing mother, as she slowly turned herself over and came to a sitting position on the bed. The dowager stood at the

143

end of the four-poster, her arms folded across her chest, her eyebrows raised in question.

"How did you know?" Hannah asked, for she was certain now her mother knew more than she wanted her to.

"Because I'm not daft," her mother replied sharply. "And because I saw you sneaking down the back stairs yesterday when you didn't know I was watching."

Hannah let out a long breath and collapsed against her pillows. "I suppose you're going to tell Evan and make certain he stops me."

Mother cocked her head sideways. "Why on earth would I do that?"

"Because what I'm doing is dangerous. What if Beeston finds me?"

"Well, I trust you're being careful."

"You do?"

The dowager moved to sit on the edge of the bed. "I know I haven't been the warmest of mothers, and I'm too old to change all of that, I assure you. But perhaps I've softened a bit. Perhaps I've seen that my children are more capable than I ever thought them to be."

Hannah almost wanted to hug the woman, but she knew Mother would never allow it, so she simply smiled and said, "Thank you, Mother."

"But I want to know exactly what you're doing. And I want to know how I can help."

"Are you certain? It is not for gently bred ladies to hear."

"My dear, I am not some green girl. Now tell me what it is you and Grace have been up to."

Hannah shifted. "If you're certain." At her mother's nod, she continued, "I have visited almost all of Beeston's former...lovers." She choked on the word again—she might never get used to saying it out loud, let alone in front of her mother.

The dowager's eyes grew round, but she remained quiet, waiting for Hannah to go on.

"Grace found them by pouring over old newspapers and Beeston's correspondence. I'm certain it's not all of them, but the list was quite long—twenty-six women—of which we've visited nineteen."

"And what is your point in doing this?" Mother wondered.

A little smile formed at the corners of Hannah's mouth —she was helpless to stop it. She'd had a plan at first, but after talking it over with the nineteen other women, she had an even better one.

"To make Beeston wish he'd never come back to England."

TWENTY-THREE

Dr. Pritchard sat in the corner of the coffee house where Plato's Assembly gathered, sipping an amber colored ale, and looking quite a bit more cheerful than last he'd seen the man. Graham strode across the space and pulled out a chair.

"Ah, there he is," Dr. Pritchard said, coming to a half stand and shoving his hand forward.

Graham shook it and then took his seat. "You look well, my friend," he said. "Seems that the country air has done you well."

"Oh, you've no idea," Pritchard laughed. "Ale?"

"Please."

The older man gestured to the waiter and then turned his attention back to Graham. "You, on the other hand, look as if you haven't slept in weeks."

"A week, to be exact," Graham admitted, as a glass of ale appeared before him. "We will get to that, I'm sure. But how did your patient fare with the babe?"

"Her condition was troubling at first, but with bed rest and constant care, I'm happy to say both mother and child are well."

"Wonderful news. It is good to have you back in London, though."

"You might not want to grow accustomed to having me here," Pritchard said, and Graham eyed him curiously. "I'm an old man, Alcott. Forty years I've been caring for people. I'm tired."

Graham nodded. It was a sad occasion, but he couldn't say he was surprised. "You deserve to live out the rest of your days peacefully," he said.

146

"Well, perhaps not peacefully." There was a glint in the old doctor's eyes. "I may have lost my mind, but for certain I've lost my heart."

Now *that* was a surprise. Dr. Pritchard was an old bachelor, always claiming he'd been too busy to take a wife. "You don't say," Graham drawled.

"She was part of the staff at Chivelesword Abbey. She caught my eye the second I saw her."

"Does she have a name?"

"Clara. Clara Smith, soon to be Pritchard."

Graham's smile spread from ear to ear. "Congratulations, my friend," he said, and he meant it, even if it did raise concern for his own situation with Hannah.

"We will marry in the parish church in Leicestershire next month, just before Christmas. We'd be honored if you could be there."

"Only if you promise to be at my wedding," Graham said, leaning forward and placing his elbows on the rough wooden table.

Pritchard's eyes grew round and wide. "You mean to say…you…but…who?"

Graham couldn't help but laugh. "You won't believe it when I tell you." He paused for a bit of dramatic effect. "The Widow Beeston."

Oh, to have a paintbrush to capture the look on the good doctor's face. He'd been rendered speechless, it seemed.

"You must be joking."

"But I'm not. And I cannot ever thank you enough for leaving Town so that I may care for her. We are quite fond of one another."

"Oh, my boy," Dr. Pritchard said, his wise, older eyes glistening. "I had feared you would end up like me, an old, lonely bachelor. This is most happy news."

Graham smiled at the man, knowing it was indeed most happy news, but also feeling deeply troubled by the shadow of

Beeston's return. "There is one small problem," he said, the words coming out slowly, reluctantly.

Pritchard's entire face wrinkled with concern. "What is that?"

Graham took a deep breath and put his face in his hands. "It seems Beeston has risen from the dead."

There was a moment's pause, and then, "Men like that always do."

"Somerset paid him to leave the country, but apparently he couldn't stay away. We don't know his plan, we just know he's here, in London. It is my belief he will attempt to reclaim his wife when we all least suspect it."

"And how is Lady Beeston doing in all of this?"

Graham shook his head, feeling helpless. "Not well. I had weaned her off the laudanum completely, she was walking —with the help of a walking stick, of course—she was happy, and now..."

"And now?"

"We're back where we started. But even worse, her sister-in-law is on her side, giving her the laudanum against my wishes. Insisting we all leave her alone. It is most painful to watch."

"And what are you doing in the meantime?"

"Searching for him."

"What will you do when you find him?"

"I would love nothing more than to drown him in the Thames," Graham admitted bluntly, at which the old man chuckled. "But I keep reminding myself I'll be of no service to Hannah if I'm locked up at Newgate. Or hung. So, to answer your question, I have no bloody idea."

Pritchard patted Graham on the arm. "I will keep my ear to the ground for you. In the meantime, take care of your bride. Give her something to live for."

Something to live for. He had hoped that something was him, but apparently it wasn't good enough. Apparently he was

HOW TO CARE FOR A LADY

no match for the despair that had befallen her. "I will try," he said finally, but his heart ached as he prayed for a miracle.

~*~

While Hannah had most desperately wanted to keep her plan as much of a secret as she could, she had to admit it was somewhat helpful to have Mother on her side. If someone had told her that her mother would be her champion a few months ago, she would have laughed in their face. But as it turned out, Mother was quite excited about the prospect of exacting revenge on the baron. Quite admittedly, he deserved it. It was just nice to know Mother thought so too, after all her years of encouraging Hannah to be a good little wife and do her duty by him. It was clear she hadn't understood the extent of Beeston's cruelty, not until the night before he shot her. The night he'd come to Somerset House screaming that she was a whore. An odd accusation since she'd barely even slept with her own husband, let alone another man.

Heavens, she couldn't wait for all this to be over with so she could be with Graham, in the truest sense of the word. He'd sparked something within her that day in her bedchamber when he'd kissed her. How she wanted more! To know what it was like to lay with someone who truly loved her and cared about her. Beeston had been...well, not terribly kind or thoughtful in the bedroom. The memories still kept her up at night sometimes, but she shook them away now. There was no time for breast beating. The plan was coming together—they had all but three girls willing to join them in the fight. They'd been too fearful, a feeling Hannah understood all too well. But she'd not fear him anymore.

Now came the hard part—the part where they would have to lure Beeston into the trap. And she had to do it quickly, before Evan and Graham found him first. Her way would be much more effective at making sure the man never stepped foot in England again, she was certain.

According to Evan—via Grace, of course—Beeston's townhome—*her* home—had been sitting empty all these

149

months, the staff having abandoned ship once she'd been shot and Beeston presumed dead. Hannah wondered why Beeston hadn't gone back there upon his return, but apparently Evan had held vigil in a bush across the street for hours and hours, waiting for the man to return home. He never did, which further propagated the idea that he may have let an apartment in Spitalfields, as Graham had heard.

That was the other way Mother had proved useful. She accompanied Graham to Hannah's bedside every morning to inquire about the investigation. Graham had no reason to believe that Hannah would do anything with the information, so he shared everything he knew. Sadly, it wasn't much. Spottings here and there, but nothing concrete, which was troubling. Hannah was starting to worry that Beeston was one step ahead of her, but *she* needed to be one step ahead of *him*. She worried every day when she went out that he might pounce upon her. She wasn't terribly strong, and with a weak leg, she wouldn't be able to outrun him or his henchmen, if he chose to hire them.

So, she did her best to hide her face and hair beneath hats and veils, but still...if the man was after her, he would stop at nothing.

"Have you heard anything, Veronica?" Hannah asked as she entered Miss Delaney's home and hung up her hat and coat on the hooks by the front door. "Veronica?"

Unusual. She ought to have been expecting her, as she had every day for the last couple weeks. John would drop her off there, and together, the two would set out to find the next girl on the list. Of course, they had exhausted the list now, but surely Veronica still planned to receive her. They still had planning to do and time was running out.

"Veronica?" She continued to call her name as she searched the downstairs rooms, her heartbeat speeding with every step she took. There was no sign of her friend on the main floor.

She stared up the staircase, and called again, "Veronica!" trying her best to tamp down the panic that was rising in her breast.

What if she was simply sleeping? Or maybe she'd even gone out. What would she think if she found Hannah lurking about the bedrooms?

But what if it was none of those things? What if...

Oh, God. She stepped onto the first step, then slowly, measuredly, climbed the rest, one by one, her heart in her throat, her hands numb from fear. Something was wrong—she could feel it in her very bones.

TWENTY-FOUR

Graham's time with Dr. Pritchard had given him new hope. Hope that he could fix Hannah again—cure her of the fear that had sent her back to the laudanum. It wasn't enough that he visited her every morning and left again, feeling dejected and hopeless. If he had no hope, how could he expect *her* to? And that was why he marched himself right back to Somerset House that afternoon. He was going to get her out of bed, remind her she was loved and that everything would turn out fine. He was going to give her hope.

The butler let him in and as he handed off his hat and coat to the man, the duchess peeked out from the drawing room, her eyes wide.

"Dr. Alcott?" she said, and Graham couldn't help but notice the high pitch of her voice.

"Your Grace," he said, with a slight bow.

"Erhm...did you forget something this morning?"

"Yes," he replied, at which point the duchess seemed to deflate in relief.

She stepped into the corridor. "Please allow me to fetch it for you."

"No, no." He held up a hand to stop her from progressing toward the stairs. "It's not an actual *thing* I've forgotten."

She stood like a statue, blinking up at him, so he went on.

"You see, I forgot to tell Hannah...that is, I forgot to remind her that..." Damn, why couldn't he find the right words? "I need to see Hannah," he finished, deciding that the young duchess didn't really need an explanation from him as to why he wanted to see his fiancée.

152

HOW TO CARE FOR A LADY

He started for the stairs, but she ran in front of him. "You can't!" she said, and now it was clear she was in a panic. But why?

"I beg your pardon?"

"That is, she's sleeping," she giggled, trying to shrug off her odd behavior. "I promised her I wouldn't let anyone interrupt."

Graham narrowed his eyes on her. She was lying, but why? What the devil was going on? "Stand aside, Your Grace."

At this, she drew herself up to her full height and shoved her nose into the air. "How dare you? This is my home, and I'll not be treated with such disrespect."

"Let him go," came another voice from behind. And older, wiser voice, that was.

"Mother! You know I can't," the duchess replied, breathless with outrage.

"He will find out one way or the other," the dowager insisted. "Let him go."

The younger woman looked as if she were going to cry as she finally stepped aside and allowed Graham to climb the stairs. He took them two at a time and then raced down the corridor until he reached Hannah's door. He didn't knock or even hesitate before he burst in to find...

Nothing? The bed was neatly made, the curtains closed. And no sign of Hannah.

"Hannah!" he called as he made his way back down the corridor. "Hannah!"

"She's not here," the dowager said as he emerged at the top of the staircase.

"Then where is she?" he demanded.

Her Grace stepped out of the drawing room again, a piece of foolscap in her hand. "Here," she said, holding it out. "You will find her here."

~*~

"Veronica?" Hannah had tried her best to slow her heart's pace as she carefully limped up the stairs of Veronica's home. Lord only knew what she'd find up here—she prayed she would merely find her new friend fast asleep in her bed.

There were three doors at the top of the landing, and Hannah had no idea what lay behind any of them. So, she chose at random, starting with the door on her left. With a trembling hand, she turned the handle and pushed the door open. Before her was a tiny room with one window and a small desk. Veronica's study, apparently. And completely empty.

She closed the door again and stared at the next one. The one in the middle. It was eerily quiet up here. The sounds of the city were muted, and Hannah's heart thumped loudly in her ears. But other than that, strange, unnerving silence.

Reluctance and curiosity warring within her, she moved to the middle door, placed her hand on the handle and then flung it open. A gasp forced itself out of her as she stared into the pleading eyes of her friend, who sat tied to a chair, her mouth gagged.

"Veronica!" she exclaimed, but the woman shook her head frantically, clearly trying to tell her something, but it was too late.

A strong arm grabbed her from behind and the sharp tip of a blade poked into her neck. *Beeston.*

"I knew this lying whore would lead you to me," Beeston spat in her ear. "And here you are, mine again, and this time...forever."

"I will nev—"

"Hush!" The knife pushed a little further into her skin. Much more and he'd draw blood. So Hannah was inclined to do as he said. "Now, you're coming with me."

"But what about Veronica?" Hannah blurted out before he could stop her.

Beeston gave a sinister laugh. "No one cares what happens to whores."

Oh, God. He planned to leave her there for dead. If only Hannah could get a message to Grace, or even John. He knew where she was. But would he dare to come looking for her?

As Beeston shoved her down the stairs, her leg began to burn. "I can't keep up this pace," she winced. "You shot me, remember?"

"You will be quiet and do as I say," he said, tightening his grip around her waist to emphasize his point.

He pushed her down the last few steps and then turned her toward the back door—the one that let out in the alleyway. There sat an unmarked carriage, black curtains drawn, and a large brute of a man sitting in the driver's seat.

Hannah stared at the coach, wide-eyed. This was it. The end. She'd never get to see Graham again to tell him how much she loved him. To tell him she was sorry and that she ought to have let him and Evan handle Beeston. That she heard every word he said to her as she lay there, pretending to be drugged and asleep.

Her heart twisted so painfully, it was almost too much to bear.

"Move!" Beeston yelled, shoving her forward and causing her to stumble over the cobblestones. Then, with the knife pressed against her back, he ushered her into the darkness, and shoved a foul-smelling cloth over her nose.

TWENTY-FIVE

Graham grabbed the paper from the duchess and scanned the address. "This isn't a very nice part of town," he remarked.

Her Grace shook her head. "No, it isn't." The young woman always had an heir of naiveté to her—the type of girl who brushed everything aside with an "Everything will turn out in the end," kind of attitude. But not now. He'd never seen her quite so serious. So frightened.

"Then why the devil is Hannah there?" He didn't mean to growl, or curse, but he was infuriated. With Hannah, with the duchess... He turned to the dowager. "Did you know about this?"

The older woman's nostrils flared just slightly as she pressed her thin lips together. "Wouldn't it be more efficient for you to question us in the carriage?"

"You're not coming with me."

"Like Hell we're not," the dowager bit back.

Graham reared back as the duchess gasped.

"There is no time for pleasantries in a situation such as this."

The woman had a point, much as he hated to admit it. But he really didn't want to be responsible for all these women in a questionable part of town.

"We should leave at once."

"Leave for where?"

"Oh, thank God," Graham said as Somerset marched into the foyer.

"What's going on?" he asked, clearly taking note of the pall that had befallen the room.

"Hannah's in trouble," Grace offered.

"I thought Hannah was asleep in her room."

"As did I." Graham handed over the piece of foolscap with the address on it. "Turns out, she's here, at this address."

The duke stared at the paper for a moment and then crumpled it in his hand. "Dammit."

"My thoughts exactly," said Graham.

Within minutes, they had all piled into one of the Somerset carriages and set off for the west end of town.

"You both have a great deal of explaining to do," Somerset said as they raced through the streets of London. "What is Bunny doing in Seven Dials?"

"It's not exactly Seven Dials," Grace said, trying to make things seem less dire than they actually were.

"Grace," the duke warned.

"Fine," she said, folding her arms across her chest with a huff. "She has been meeting with all of Beeston's former..." She shifted beside the duke and her cheeks flushed a bright pink.

"Lovers," the dowager finished for her with a roll of her eyes.

"Lovers?" Graham repeated, certain he'd heard her wrong.

"For what purpose?" asked Somerset.

The two women looked at each other and shared some kind of unspoken communication.

"We can't tell you," the duchess finally supplied.

"Like hell you can't!" Somerset was seething now. "I command you both to tell us what is going on."

The dowager waved her hand lazily in the air. "Stand down, Somerset," she said. "You cannot command us to do anything. Hannah made us swear to secrecy. Only *she* can tell you her plan...if she so chooses."

Graham sought to be the calm and sensible one in this situation, so he leaned forward, elbows on knees, and made his plea. "I respect your oath to Hannah," he said, keeping his tone even. "But now her life is in danger, could you not make an exception?"

157

The dowager turned her beady eyes on him. "We don't yet know that her life is in danger. Once we have confirmed that, we will consider if you need to know the plan."

Damned infuriating woman. Somerset looked as if he wanted to toss her from the carriage window. Graham was of a similar mind. And then he'd deliver a proper scolding to his intended when they found her.

If they found her.

They rode in silence the rest of the way, Somerset brooding, the women looking properly terrified, and Graham, praying to whatever deity might be willing to help him in this moment. He just wanted his Hannah to be safe.

The carriage pulled to a stop what seemed like hours later on a side street in Covent Garden, indeed on the edge of Seven Dials. What the devil was Hannah thinking coming here?

Graham and Somerset hopped down from the carriage, and then the duchess attempted to step down as well, but Somerset halted her mid-step.

"Where do you think you're going?" he bit out.

One would have to be an idiot not to see the fire and determination in the woman's eyes. "To find my sister-in-law."

"You and Mother will stay in the carriage."

"I don't think so." The dowager was on the sidewalk beside them, and both Graham and Somerset stared at her, agape. "There is a door on the other side, you know? Now let her down. We're all going together."

"It's bad enough Hannah has been deceiving and defying us, must you insist on doing the same?"

The dowager stared at her son for a long moment, and Graham almost wondered if she'd had a change of heart, until she said simply, "Yes. Now let her down."

Somerset hesitated.

"There are no locks on these doors. Even if we stay now, we will only get out in a few minutes' time."

158

That was true. They had no real way of keeping them inside.

"Fine." Somerset flipped his hand over and helped his wife from the carriage. "But you will do as we say, is that understood?"

"Perfectly," the duchess replied haughtily.

And then they all walked to the door belonging to one Ms. Veronica Delaney.

TWENTY-SIX

Hannah blinked her eyes open, but all she could see was black. Oh, God. Where was she? What had happened to her? Panic settled in her breast as the memories came flooding back. Veronica, bound and gagged. The cold steel of a knife against her throat.

Beeston.

She couldn't remember anything after that. Was she still in Veronica's townhome? And what did Beeston plan to do with her now that he'd captured her?

Hannah swallowed down the tears that threatened to overtake her. She had to keep her wits about her, keep her mind sharp.

Oh, yes. There were stairs, and a carriage. But nothing after that.

She blinked some more as her eyes adjusted to the darkness, and she tried to sit up, but her head hurt too much. It was a similar feeling to what she felt after too much laudanum. She wanted to sleep forever. But she couldn't. Not with Beeston near. Who knew what he'd do to her in her sleep. Perhaps he'd already done it.

That thought made her stomach churn. She had to figure a way out of this. But first, she had to figure out where she was in the first place.

As painful as it was, she pushed herself up to a sitting position. She was on some kind of feather bed that sat on the floor, and the ends of the feathers poked through the rough cotton, making it decidedly uncomfortable. Though she supposed he could have just left her on the cold, hard floor, so there was that.

160

"Ah, you're awake," came the baneful voice of her husband. The sound alone made her want to toss up her breakfast.

"Ah, you're alive," she replied in the same tone of voice.

"Surprise!" He giggled with maniacal glee.

"Where are you?" Hannah demanded, hating that she was rendered helpless in the darkness.

"You would love to know, wouldn't you?" Beeston hissed, his tone changing suddenly.

"I only—" But before she could finish, a pair of foul-tasting lips pressed against hers, followed by a pair of hands that sought to take liberties with her person.

He was strong, always had been, and no matter how she struggled, she couldn't get him off her. She hated the panic that fluttered in her chest. The tears that sprung from her eyes. Those things would only embolden him, the sick bastard. If only she could get enough leverage to kick him where it would truly hurt him. But alas, there was no such leverage from her position beneath him on the feathered bed.

"Did you miss me?" he hissed, pulling away, his breath hot and foul on her face.

"Like one misses a toothache," Hannah spat back. She ought to have held her tongue, but if he planned to kill her, being kind probably wouldn't make a difference.

He pressed himself against her again, grinding his manhood against her leg—the one he'd shot. She winced against the pain, willing herself not to cry, telling herself she'd been through worse, clinging to the hope that Grace would eventually let the others know that she'd been gone too long. That something was wrong.

"Why?" she whimpered, and she hadn't even realized she'd said it out loud until Beeston paused.

"What's that, love?"

She hated when he called her that, as if he'd ever loved her.

"Why did you come back?" she finished. She wanted to know what his plans were for her. For them.

"Ah, well...my reasons are two-fold, actually. Your brother was kind enough to give me quite a sum to go away the first time—I figure he'll give me even more this time in hopes that I'll stay away for good."

"And will you?" Hannah wondered.

His hand gently caressed her face—a gesture in stark contrast to his words. "It won't matter to you, my lady," he whispered. Then he pressed himself upon her again, and Hannah understood. Her end was near.

TWENTY-SEVEN

The door was unlocked, the modest townhome completely silent. Graham hated the feeling he had as the four of them searched each room, looking for a sign, anything that would tell them Hannah had been there.

"Nothing," Somerset said as they met in the first floor foyer again, then he gestured up the staircase before them. "Shall we?"

Graham nodded and started up first, leading the way to the top of the stairs. Only as he stood on the landing could he hear the faintest of sounds. A whimper, a cry...hope fluttered in his breast, and he burst into the room from whence the sound came.

"Hannah!" he cried, flinging the door wide, but then he stopped when he realized the woman bound to the overturned chair wasn't Hannah.

The duchess pushed past him. "Miss Delaney!" she cried, kneeling at the woman's side and pulling the gag from her mouth. "Oh, you poor thing."

Graham and Somerset sprang into action, untying the coarse ropes from her hands and feet and then helping her to the bed. She was a sturdy woman with dark hair and eyes that belied her young age. She'd seen far too much in her years, Graham suspected.

The dowager put herself to good use, dampening a cloth and bringing it to Miss Delaney. She pressed it against her mouth and then her forehead, sweeping her cheeks and finally her neck, where she let the cloth rest, while Somerset began to question her.

"Who did this to you?"

The woman's lip trembled as she spoke. "Lord Beeston."

163

Graham had hoped that wasn't the case, but of course deep down he'd known it was. "Tell us exactly what happened."

"He surprised me," she whimpered. "I didn't know he was here. And then all of a sudden, he had me pinned down, tying ropes around my wrists. Swore he'd kill me if I screamed."

"Did he hurt you?" Graham asked, picking up her wrists to examine the burns, praying he'd otherwise left her alone.

She shook her dark curls. "No. It wasn't me he was after."

Graham's heart stopped for what felt like far too long before it sped to a gallop. "Where is she?" he growled, unable to control the fury that was building inside of him.

The woman trembled and tears leaked from her eyes. "I don't know," she whispered. "He knocked me unconscious before he took her—that must be how I ended up on the floor."

"Dammit," Somerset hissed.

"Did he hurt her?" Graham asked.

Miss Delaney swallowed over a lump in her throat as she stared into Graham's eyes. "I don't know," she said. "But he had a knife to her throat."

The whole room fell silent and still. Graham clenched his fists at his side.

"Dr. Alcott?" the duchess said, tentatively.

"If he touches one hair on her head, I swear I'll kill him," Graham growled.

"Not if I get to him first," Somerset said.

"The two of you must calm down if you wish to rescue Hannah from the likes of Beeston."

"Calm down?" Somerset gaped at his mother.

"*Think*," she continued. "Someone spotted him in Spitalfields, didn't you say?"

HOW TO CARE FOR A LADY

"Yes," Graham confirmed, trying to steady his breathing. "But that's all we have. A small apartment in Spitalfields. We don't even know if it's his."

"Isn't it worth a try?" the duchess chimed in. "I will stay here with Miss Delaney—"

"No!"

All eyes turned to Miss Delaney.

"That is, I wish to go with you."

Somerset held up a hand. "You've been through quite a trauma. I don't think it's such a good idea."

"But I've been there!"

"Been where?" the dowager asked.

"To that apartment. Long ago, and it was after dark. I can't guarantee I will recognize it, but I can try."

Somerset turned to Graham.

Graham shrugged. "She may be our only hope."

"Then let us not waste time." The duchess and Miss Delaney stood from the edge of the bed and together, the five of them made for the stairs.

~*~

They arrived in Spitalfields nearly an hour later, thanks to congestion on the roadways. With every minute that passed, Graham became more and more worried. What would Beeston do to her? What was he doing to her now? He had to push the thoughts from his mind before his imagination ran away with him. With any luck, the man just wanted her for ransom, and a heavy purse would persuade him to let her go.

A shiver chased up Graham's spine. He had a feeling that would not be the case at all. Everything he'd heard about Beeston told him he was a beast of a man with very little concern for anyone but himself, let alone a woman whom he deemed his property.

That thought made Graham cringe. It wasn't an uncommon thought in the world—the idea that a wife was one's property—and yet he couldn't seem to wrap his mind around it. She was just as much human as he was, and he

165

would treat her as such. Sure, they had different strengths, but they were meant to compliment one another, not dominate one over the other.

"There," came Miss Delaney's voice, snapping Graham from his thoughts. He glanced out the window to see they'd come to a stop very near to where Plato's Assembly gathered. Wouldn't that be ironic if the man had been hiding out just upstairs from the coffee house?

"That one?" Somerset asked, pointing to a building that held a bookshop on the level of the street, and what appeared to be housing above.

"One of these, for sure," the woman replied.

The duke turned to his wife. "You will stay here this time—there will be no arguments."

Her Grace wisely didn't argue this time, and for that, Graham was grateful. There wasn't time for discussion. He wanted to get Hannah out of there as soon as was possible.

"Mother," Somerset said, turning to the dowager.

"I will stay with Grace. Go, hurry."

Graham scrambled out of the carriage after Miss Delaney, who led them to the door she recognized.

"I think this is the one. I can't be entirely certain, but I seem to remember this blue paint."

"We will begin the search," Somerset said. "You wait here and maintain a lookout."

The woman nodded and then Graham and Somerset pushed through the door and started up the stairs.

TWENTY-EIGHT

How long had she been here? It felt like days, or maybe just hours. She had no way of knowing, since the room was pitch black. Beeston had left some time ago, but it had been almost as dark in the next room when he'd opened the door to leave. So it was difficult to know what time of day it was. Hannah had dozed off several times—it was impossible not to in such darkness. And now she'd completely lost track of time.

Deep breaths. She relied on them to keep her calm as she waited.

Waited for what? Death? Salvation? *Graham*?

Her heart ached as she thought of him. Was he worried about her? Did he know the truth now? That she hadn't really been taking the laudanum? That it had all been a silly, foolish ruse to trap Beeston and give him a dose of his own medicine?

What a mutton-headed ninny she was! And now, she might never see Graham again.

The sound of muffled voices reached her ears—in the darkness, she heard everything. Were they in the apartment—if that was even what this was? Or were they...

Evan. That was his voice. She'd know that growl anywhere. They had come for her, but would they be able to retrieve her without a fight? What if someone got hurt? She'd never forgive herself if something happened to Evan or Graham.

Hannah fumbled around in the dark. She hadn't dared do so before, but knowing they were so close, she felt emboldened. She felt her way across the floor, on hands and knees, toward the sounds of their voices. They were getting louder, they pounded on the outside door. Would Beeston open it?

167

She reached the wall and ran her hands up it, trying to find a door, a handle—

"Ah!" Hannah went flying backward, landing on her bottom, her face throbbing from whatever had been shoved into it.

"You stupid woman!" Beeston hissed as he scrambled into the room, shutting the door behind him. "Where are you?"

Hannah wanted to laugh. He really thought she was going to speak and give away her position? No, she had a better idea.

He was stomping about the room, clearly looking for her—she could barely make out his shadow—but if she moved just a bit to her left...

Beeston went tumbling over her in the darkness, crashing to the floor, taking furniture with him, in a chorus of grunts and grumbling. "Hannah!" he growled. "I'll kill you."

And she knew he would. Which was why she had to get out of there. With only a general idea of where the door was, she lunged toward it in the darkness, finding the handle and yanking it open. The rest of the place was dim, but at least she could see where the devil she was going now.

"Don't you dare!" Beeston was after her, and with her bad leg, she had a disadvantage. But she had to try to get to the door. To Graham.

"I'm here!" she cried out as she hobbled through the apartment, overturning a small table and then a chair into the path behind her.

The door was within reach. She was going to make it.

But just as she reached out for the doorknob, Beeston's hand closed around her wrist, yanking her backward with a sharp jerk, while at the same time, two men busted through the door in a cloud of dust and broken wood.

"Graham!" she cried, her heart soaring at the sight of him. Even covered in dust, he was the most handsome man she'd ever seen.

HOW TO CARE FOR A LADY

"Hannah!" He began to step toward her, but halted just before Hannah felt the cool barrel of Beeston's gun meet her temple.

~*~

Dear God. Graham had never been so terrified in all his life.

No, that wasn't true, was it? He'd felt this before...the day his parents had perished in the fire. He'd just stood there, much like he was doing now, completely helpless. Unable to save them. Knowing that if he went into that burning building, he'd lose his life too and leave Daphne all alone in the world.

And now he was the one terrified of being left alone in the world. He couldn't imagine life without her, without his Hannah. There had to be something they could do. But what? The man had a gun pointed at her head, and heaven knew he wouldn't hesitate to shoot if Graham or Evan made a wrong move.

He met Hannah's eyes, clouded in fear, shimmering with tears and longing. Longing to be set free, no doubt. Her lip began to tremble, but she was trying to be brave. He could see that. She hadn't given up. Not yet.

"Beeston," the duke said, his tone cajoling. "This isn't necessary. Put down the gun."

"You would love that, wouldn't you?" the man spat back, and Graham realized in that moment how deranged he was. The man was mad.

But Somerset ignored him. "Look here," he said, pulling a coin purse from inside his coat and dangling it in the air. "You would never run out. It is far more than I offered you the first time."

"You think I can be bought with a bit of coin?"

"A bit?" the duke raised his brows. "This is far more than any person truly needs."

"Yes, but it's not really what I want." He pressed the gun harder into Hannah's temple, eliciting a gasp from her.

169

Graham's stomach churned. He was going to shoot her. Even just a slip of his finger and—

The shot was deafening. It rent the air, sending Graham and Somerset to the ground, confusedly trying to make sense of what had happened. Dear God. *Hannah*!

TWENTY-NINE

It took Hannah longer than it ought to have to realize she was still alive. Her heart was pounding in her ears, her stomach twisting so violently with fear that she doubled over and fell to the ground. Right beside her husband.

Her dead husband.

"My God," she whispered, trying to understand what had happened, but nothing was making sense.

She looked across the room to where Graham and Evan both sat on their knees, seemingly as stymied as she was, their gazes focused on something behind her. Slowly, Hannah turned to look behind her. There, in all her courtesan glory, stood Veronica, a smoking gun in her hand, a smug look of satisfaction on her face.

"Veronica?" Hannah mumbled, in awe of the woman standing before her. "How did you...?"

"It's not the first time I've had to scale a wall," she said with a wink. "Are you all right?"

Hannah looked down at herself to assess if there'd been any damage. "I think so," she replied.

And then, before she could make another move, a pair of arms gathered her up and pulled her tightly against a strong, lean body. She melted into Graham, the tears she'd been holding back flowing freely now. It would take a while for her to realize she was truly safe, truly free. But for now, she would revel in the warmth of her intended.

"We heard a gun shot!" Grace appeared in the doorway, her eyes wild, her breathing belabored from clearly running up the stairs.

"Grace, you're going to tax yourself and the babe," the dowager scolded, coming up behind her. "And look..." She gestured through the broken doorway into the small apartment. "Everything is just as it should be. Well done, Miss Delaney."

Hannah could hardly believe her mother, of all people, was offering praise to a woman of the night. It seemed people could change after all. Just not Beeston. What an act he'd put on for her that day in her chamber, seemingly broken and guilt-ridden. All lies. But he'd never be able to tell another.

Hannah swiped at her eyes and looked at the dead form of Beeston lying on the floor. Only then did it occur to her that Miss Delaney could pay royally for her crime, no matter that it was in defense of another.

"Veronica," she said, pushing away from Graham and coming to her feet. "No one must know what you've done."

The woman, confident and buxom, sauntered to Hannah. "You needn't worry about me, my lady. I've always taken care of myself."

"I'm sure you have but—"

"It will look like suicide." Evan came up beside her and gestured to Beeston. He still held his own gun in his hand.

"And what about the door?" Grace put in. "I think that makes it look a bit more like murder, don't you?"

"We had to break in after we heard a gunshot," Graham said, and Hannah smiled up at him as she reached for his hand.

"Of course you did," she said.

"Then it is settled. We all agree on what happened?"

Everyone nodded, and then, one by one, they filed out of the little apartment. Graham held tightly to Hannah's hand as they stepped through the open doorway, and she didn't bother to spare even one last glance for the man she'd called husband.

THIRTY

Graham arrived at Somerset House the next morning, the same time he always did, eager to see his bride. As he divested himself of his greatcoat and hat, he realized that, in spite of the earth-shattering events of yesterday, the house was surprisingly back to normal. The servants bustled about, and he could hear the duchess and the dowager chatting in the front parlor. Yet, there seemed to be an air of lightness to the whole scene where there had once been a dark shadow hanging overhead.

He didn't bother to announce himself to the ladies—there was only one lady he wished to see this morning. So he bounded up the stairs two at a time and practically ran down the corridor until he reached her door. He wasn't sure why he was so nervous—they were in love, to be married soon, and had shared some intimacies already. But something about this felt different. Perhaps it was knowing that she was finally, truly free to be his. That there was no more threat to their happiness, be it man or medicine.

He turned the knob and poked his head through the door. "Good morning," he said, smiling at the vision of her propped up in bed, a large tray of food on her lap. "How is my favorite patient?"

She beamed back at him. Even with her mouth full of food, she was beautiful, radiant. His dream come true.

"You shouldn't play favorites with your patients, you know?" she teased, her dark eyes glistening in the morning light.

Graham closed the door behind him and moved to the bed, placing his bag on the floor and taking a seat beside her. "You will have to find it in your heart to forgive me, but I simply cannot help myself."

"Well," she giggled, "perhaps I can allow it just this once."

He couldn't wait any longer. He lifted up off the seat and placed his hands on either side of her on the bed before leaning down to capture her sweet lips. "Someone's been eating sweet biscuits for breakfast," he murmured.

"I would offer you some," she said, her voice lower now, seductive, "but then you wouldn't be able to kiss me."

He needed no more encouragement. He would forego a lifetime of sweet biscuits in order to be able to kiss her and never stop.

Their tongues intertwined. She was so soft, so perfect. Everything he'd ever dreamed of. Hannah, his beautiful, beautiful bride. But suddenly, kisses were not enough.

He pulled away and took the tray from her lap, placing it on top of the dresser. Then he began to divest himself of his clothing—he couldn't do it fast enough. And Hannah watched, lust and desire infusing her smile, lighting her eyes.

"Do you plan to have your way with me right now?" she asked, hope in her tone.

"If it pleases my lady."

"Oh, it pleases her."

With one last tug of his cravat, it came free and he tossed it to the floor, along with his boots, pants, and shirt, leaving him clad in only his undergarments. The proof of his desire straining against his drawers.

Hannah patted the bed, inviting him to join her, and he did so with great alacrity. He climbed atop her, showering her with kisses, with love.

~*~

Never in her life had Hannah imagined lovemaking could be so...*loving*. But Graham was so gentle, so caring, so concerned with her pleasure that it nearly made her cry. How was she so fortunate to have this man in her bed, in her life? After so many years of hating her life, hating herself, it felt like the most wonderful dream. A dream from which she hoped she never awakened.

His hands caressed her as their tongues danced with one another. Everything was so soft and wet and sweet, and Hannah wanted more. She'd never had the opportunity to be adventurous in bed. Her encounters had consisted of Beeston waking her in the dead of night, drunk and slobbering all over her. Hardly the stuff of dreams. But this...*this* was a dream. And Hannah was about to make Graham's dreams come true, too.

She pushed against him, their eyes locked as she traded places with him, forcing him to the bed as she climbed atop him.

"Dear God," he whispered. "Have I died?"

"You are about to," Hannah purred. "In the Shakespearean sense, of course."

This seemed to fuel his fire, and Graham reached up to pull her down to him, kissing her like she'd never been kissed in her life. Loving her like she'd never been loved.

And then, Hannah slipped herself over him, reveling in the glorious desire that filled her body and soul. It was enough to make her cry tears of joy, of relief, but they were short lived, replaced with sheer ecstasy as they became one, in a perfect rhythm. Until neither could hold back any longer.

Hannah exploded inside, the heat and wonder overcoming her, transcending any earthly feeling she'd ever experienced. And then Graham was with her, holding her closer, tighter. Filling her, pressing further than she thought possible. Loving her harder than she ever could have imagined.

When the fire had died to a dull ember, Hannah collapsed atop him, and then he rolled her to the side, so they lay face-to-face, nose-to-nose. She couldn't wipe the smile from her lips, no matter how hard she tried.

"I suppose you will have to marry me now," she teased.

Graham gave a little laugh. "I suppose I shall," he replied. "And I shall never, ever complain about it."

They kissed again, briefly, just a simple gesture of love, rather than a rabid one of passion.

Then Graham turned serious. "If you ever want to talk about what happened—"

"I don't," Hannah cut him off. "It was nothing worse than I endured being married to him. Well, aside from the part where he put a gun to my head. That was entirely new, but... thank heavens for Miss Delaney."

"Indeed." Graham smiled at her. "You are an extraordinary woman."

"Perhaps I had to be for such an extraordinary man to love me."

THIRTY-ONE

"Ah! There you are!"

Hannah glanced up to find Grace standing in the doorway of the parlor, all dressed and ready to leave for some sort of fete, it would seem. "Yes, and I've been here for quite some time. Have you been looking for me?"

"Well, not for very long, admittedly," Grace said, moving toward her. "I went to your chambers first, but Alice said I'd find you here."

"And why were you looking for me in the first place?"

"Oh, yes, erm..." Grace's eyes darted about, a clear sign she was about to tell a lie. "I was hoping you would join me on a little shopping trip. I'd love your opinion on the hat I had commissioned."

"A hat you say?" Hannah confirmed, wondering what was really going on.

"Mm-hm." Her sister-in-law wouldn't look her in the eye.

"Well..." Hannah sighed and sat back in her seat. "I had planned to watch the birds from the verandah today, and maybe chat with the worms..."

"Oh, you are incorrigible since you fell in love!" Grace punched her fists to her hips, finally meeting Hannah's gaze.

"Will you tell me what's really going on?"

"I can't, but I need you to trust me."

"Trust *you*," she teased.

"Oh, for heaven's sake, just go with the girl!" the dowager called from across the room. Hannah had forgotten her mother was even there.

"Thank you," Grace called over her shoulder.

"Fine." Hannah stood, smiling amusedly. She would have gone anyway, since her curiosity was indubitably peaked now. "May I retrieve my pelisse?"

"Already done. Baldrick is waiting for you in the foyer."

"Well, then, I can't wait to see this *hat*."

She followed Grace out the door and into the carriage. Her sister-in-law insisted on closing the curtains so Hannah couldn't see where they were going and ruin the surprise. Hannah quipped that she'd been to the hatmaker's before, but Grace didn't find it quite as amusing as she did.

Finally, the carriage pulled to a stop, at which point Grace asked Hannah to turn around.

"Turn around?"

"I have to blindfold you."

"*Blindfold* me?"

"Will you *please* stop being so difficult?"

Hannah laughed, but turned around anyway, allowing Grace to put a blindfold over her eyes and then lead her from the carriage. Hannah tried to take in the sounds and smells around her—they certainly weren't in Mayfair anymore, but it really could have been anywhere in London.

"Three steps up," Grace said. "One, two, three. There. Now right this way."

They were inside now. Inside of what, she didn't know. And then, all at once, light flooded her eyes as a chorus of *Surprise!* rang in her ears.

Hannah blinked, trying to take in the scene before her. Good heavens. They were all here. Here in Veronica's little parlor. All the women she'd met with. All the women that had had the unfortunate experience of sleeping with her former husband, gathered in one place, smiling at her, some with tears in their eyes. It was so overwhelming that Hannah struggled to take in air.

"What—what is this?" she breathed.

Grace took her hand and squeezed it tightly. "This," her sister-in-law said, "is for you."

"But I don't understand." And truly, she didn't.

Veronica stepped forward, her startling blue eyes filled with light and hopefulness. "You have been through so much—endured far too many years with that vile man—and yet you have shown nothing but kindness to all of us." She gestured to the women at large. "We wanted to find a way to honor you, to turn your struggle into a way to help other women who may seek asylum from a man who might harm her. Or for women who want a different life from the one they may have fallen into. Like many of us here." She stepped aside to allow two of the women to come forward. They held a sign between them that read HANNAH'S HOME.

Hannah couldn't breathe. The lump in her throat was nearly choking her.

"Evan and I have purchased a large townhome not far from here," Grace added. "Large enough to house at least twenty women at a time. And your own Dr. Alcott has agreed to make certain all the women are well cared for and healthy."

Hannah cast her gaze to Grace. "Graham?"

Grace nodded.

"But..." She had so many questions, she didn't even know where to begin. So she said simply, "I am overwhelmed. And honored."

"Come." Grace took her by the hand and began to lead her out of the room and toward the back of the house. "We've planned a little something for you."

Hannah couldn't imagine what was happening, but when Grace opened the door to the garden, she saw that it had been transformed. Where it used to be a dismal place overrun with weeds, there were flowers and healthy plants everywhere, benches and tables, upon which were plates of cakes and biscuits and sandwiches...a garden party in a lovely little enchanted garden.

"It's magnificent," Hannah breathed. "But you didn't have to do all this for me."

"They wanted to," Grace replied. "After Beeston ruined your plans for him, well, they didn't want to leave it at that. They wanted you to know that they were willing to stand by you, no matter what."

"I don't deserve all this."

"No," Grace said. "You deserve far more. But this will have to do."

THIRTY-TWO

As far as wedding days went, Graham imagined there had never been a more perfect one in all of history. Snow was gently falling outside the stained glass windows of St. George's, and the whole town smelled of cinnamon and clove. The church was decorated in garlands of holly, heralding the joyous holiday. Christmas Eve would never be the same — it would forever be the happiest day of his life.

Graham stood at the front of the church, Somerset and Dr. Pritchard on one side of him, the minister on the other, while Her Grace, the Duchess of Somerset, made her way down the aisle clad in dark green satin with a small bouquet of white roses in her hands.

The music changed once the duchess reached the pulpit, and the congregation stood as Hannah, his beautiful bride, appeared at the back of the nave.

Graham could hardly catch his breath. She was a vision in cream and silver, like a shimmering angel, walking toward him so slowly, Graham worried she would never get there. She had a smile for him, and for everyone she passed. The entire Wetherby family had turned out for the occasion, considering themselves extended family now. All the women from Hannah's Home were in attendance as well — a situation that would surely be mentioned in the gossip columns tomorrow. There was Daphne and Wolf, Garrick and Tilly. And, of course, the dowager, who stood in the front row, beaming as her daughter walked toward her down the aisle.

Graham had always thought it was impossible to change people — to truly amend their nature — but the dowager had proved him wrong. While she was still a blunt and entitled old woman, she was somehow softer now. Kinder. Most

181

certainly not the woman he had met many months ago when he'd first arrived at Somerset House.

When Hannah arrived at the pulpit, her gaze met with his, loving and longing, and oh, so happy. The smile on her face matched his, and they joined hands, ready to finally become man and wife.

EPILOGUE

Michael & Elizabeth

"You're shaking like a leaf."

Elizabeth Wetherby looked up at her husband, Michael, and forced a smile. "I know," she said, and then turned her attention back to the passing scenery.

"Are you cold?"

She smiled and shook her head, remembering a similar conversation from more than four years ago when they'd been traveling to Scotland. Now they were traveling home, to England, for the first time in a very long time. In some ways it felt like forever, and in others it felt as if they'd never left. But they had left, thanks to the scandal Michael and his twin, Andrew, had caused. Lizzie was never supposed to marry Michael—it was supposed to be Andrew. But seeing as he'd fallen in love with her cousin...

Oh, it was no use going over all of it in her head again. She'd done so a thousand times, and it didn't change the outcome. Not that she wanted it to. She loved Michael. She just hoped the *ton* had forgotten how they'd come to be man and wife.

"You know I'm not cold," Lizzie finally replied.

His warm hand wrapped around her gloved fingers. "You don't have to be nervous, my love."

"Simple for you to say," she retorted. "You've seen your family some in the last few years. I've barely seen mine at all." A fresh batch of butterflies started beating about in her stomach. "Oh, heavens, do I look all right?"

Michael reached up and stilled the hand that had begun to fuss with her hair. "You look stunning...as always."

"Please don't patronize me now. I'm in no mood for your cajoling." A wide grin broke out on Michael's lips, and Elizabeth fought the urge to laugh herself. "Stop that!"

"You want me to stop smiling at you?"

"Yes!"

Michael shook his head. "I'm sorry, but I can't." He continued to gaze at her with that adorable, boyish grin. It encompassed love and mischief all at the same time, and it completely unarmed Elizabeth.

She turned her head sharply away and focused once again on the familiar landscape outside. "Then I shan't be able to look at you." They were getting closer to London—it wouldn't be much longer before they were ensconced in her family's townhouse, making merry with her brothers and sisters and— "I know you're still looking at me!" she exclaimed without turning back to Michael.

Her husband burst into laughter and then drew her backwards into his arms. She leaned against him, unable to resist his charms anymore.

"This poor child won't be able to get anything past you, will she?" He placed a hand to her stomach and then abruptly pulled it away. "Good God, what was that? Are you all right?"

Elizabeth laughed. "Of course I'm all right, you ninny. Why wouldn't I be?"

He tentatively put his hand back to her belly. "You mean it's supposed to do that?"

"Yes, *it* is supposed to do that," she said. "It is a human, after all. And last I checked, humans tended to move about, even when confined to small spaces, like this blasted carriage."

"Can you make it happen again?"

"Can you make the sun shine more brightly?"

"Touché."

Silence fell over them as the carriage crossed the Thames, headed for the city. Elizabeth closed her eyes and took a deep breath, taking comfort in the gentle way Michael caressed her stomach.

"Do you think anyone remembers?" she asked, her voice quiet.

"The question is not will they remember. The question is will they care? And the answer is most assuredly *no*."

"How can you be so sure?" Michael was always so sure of everything; it made Elizabeth feel most inadequate in the area of certainty.

"It's been four years, Beth." He turned her slightly and tipped her chin up. After all this time, she still couldn't help but get lost in those deep, brown eyes. "The only thing anyone cares about is having you back home."

Elizabeth wanted to cry at his tenderness. Well, truth be known, she wanted to cry at everything these days. It was deuced annoying that. How in the world did her sisters-in-law carry so many children and not dry themselves up completely?

"Thank you," she said to Michael, blinking back her tears. "That does make me feel better."

"Good, because we're here."

~*~

Michael knew his wife was a bundle of nerves about returning to London for the holiday, so he decided not to mention to her how nervous *he* was. She would only wonder at his nervousness and find more reasons to be nervous herself. That was something neither of them needed, especially considering her delicate emotional state of late. He would be thrilled once the baby finally arrived...although Beth had done a nice job of watering the household plants over the last few months.

As the carriage blessedly pulled to a stop in front of his brother's townhouse, he turned to face his wife. "Are you ready?" he asked.

Beth smiled. "I'm not sure it would matter if I wasn't. It's not like we could turn back now." She gave a little nod toward the window and Michael turned to see his sister-in-law barreling down the sidewalk toward them.

Phoebe Wetherby, Marchioness of Eastleigh, looked every bit the marchioness in her midnight blue gown, with her auburn hair styled to perfection. A small boy followed in her wake. His thick, dark hair and large brown eyes made it obvious he was the progeny of Phoebe and his brother, Benjamin.

"I can't believe it!" she exclaimed as Michael helped Beth down from the carriage. "You didn't say anything about being *enceinte!*"

A wide smile broke out on Elizabeth's lips as Phoebe gathered her in a hug. "I wanted it to be a surprise," she said. "And I knew if I told you or Katherine that the entire town would know before we ever arrived."

"I will breech no argument to that," Phoebe replied, laughing. "Come, come. You'll catch your deaths out here."

She led them up the walk after a few brief instructions for the horses to be taken to the mews and the trunks to be delivered to the green guest chambers. The butler awaited them in the entrance and wasted no time in divesting them of their outer clothes.

"Come," Phoebe said, taking Elizabeth by the arm. "I've had the fire stoked and food set out for you in the drawing room."

Michael followed behind, grateful for his sister-in-law's gracious hospitality. He loved their home in Scotland—it was where they would raise their family and grow old together. But being in London again felt good, and he would rest easier knowing their child would be born here, rather than in their remote little village in the highlands.

"Well, well, the prodigal son returns."

Michael spun on his heel just before he reached the drawing room to find his brother at the other end of the corridor, handing off his coat to a footman. He was as imposing as ever with his broad shoulders and tall stature. His dark Wetherby hair was starting to sprout a bit of silver, making him seem even more distinguished than before.

"What ho, old man!" Michael shouted as they made their way toward one another. They embraced and then Benjamin took him by the shoulders and pushed him back so he could look at him.

"We thought you'd never come home," Ben said, a great deal of warmth to his tone. "It is good to see you, brother."

"We couldn't stay away forever, could we? Besides, we have more than one good reason to be here now."

Ben's brows knit together in confusion. "I haven't a clue what you're talking about."

Michael smiled as they turned to head toward the drawing room. "You will soon enough."

As if Phoebe were a magpie with a homing instinct, she emerged into the corridor at that exact moment. "Benjamin, you're home!" She placed a hurried kiss to his cheek and then burst out, "You won't believe it—Lizzie is *enceinte!*"

Ben turned on Michael with a wide smile. "I knew you could do it, little brother!" he said, clapping him on the back. "Let me congratulate your wife and then we'll retire to my study for port and cigars. This calls for a celebration."

Chloe & Andrew

"Good heavens, what chaos!" Chloe Wetherby stood in the doorway to her children's nursery, dumbfounded by the mess they'd made. And by the fact that her sister, Cassandra, had allowed them to make such a mess. "Cassie, I thought you were watching them."

Her little sister's curls bounced frantically as she bounded across the room. "Oh, I have been, Clo! We've been having a grand time defeating Napolean's army, haven't we?"

Two chubby faces peered up at them with wide smiles. Four-year-old Samantha wore a hat made of paper upon her head and a mustache made of—

"Is that chocolate on your lip?" Chloe asked, trying not to laugh.

"Mm-hm, and it is delicious!"

Benedict, who was not even a year yet, sat giggling amidst a sea of pillows.

"Well, we're going to be late for dinner if we don't hurry. What a blessedly inconvenient time for Martha to take sick to her bed." She picked up Benedict and stood by the door. "Cassie, please dress Sam for dinner and wash the chocolate off her face. I will send Deborah to help you dress when she's done helping me. Good heavens, how did Mother handle six children with no help whatsoever?"

"Mother never had to dress us for fancy dinners," Cassie rejoined as she led Sam through the door into the corridor.

"Well, that's true, isn't it?"

Her sister and daughter skipped toward the staircase. With Benedict on her hip, Chloe followed them to the children's bedchambers. As she began to dress her sweet little boy, she realized her hands were shaking. So much so that she could hardly loop the buttons through the holes on his shirt.

She took a deep breath. Her nerves were on edge. She hadn't seen her cousin in so very long. What would it be like?

Had she changed very much? By her letters it would seem Lizzie—or Beth, as Michael had taken to calling her—had grown up quite a bit, no longer consumed with frivolities and gossip. But would seeing Chloe remind her of what had happened? Of her horrific betrayal?

Chloe hated that she'd done it, but in the end, she couldn't feel badly about it. She'd fallen in love with Andrew, and according to Shakespeare, one could not help such a thing. Besides, she and Andrew had two beautiful children together, so any regrets she might have had before were now gone altogether.

Well, all but one. She did regret the rift that had formed between Lizzie and herself.

"There we are!" she said, smiling down at her son's angelic face. "As handsome as ever."

"I'm ready too, Mama!"

Chloe swung around to see Samantha fully dressed in a white dress with lace trim, a thick satin sash about the waist, her hair partially up with a mass of dark curls cascading over her shoulders. Chloe beamed at her daughter.

"You look lovely, my dear. Now, Cassie, go and get ready quickly, then hurry back so you can look after the children while I finish getting ready myself."

"Why don't *I* look after the children?"

Chloe looked up to find her husband in the doorway—her knight on a white charger. "When did you get home?" she wondered as he crossed the room towards her.

He leaned down and planted a kiss on her cheek before ruffling Benedict's hair. "Just now. But I'm desperate for a spot of tea."

A little gasp came from the other side of the room. "Papa! I can serve you tea!" Samantha cried, her eyes alight with excitement.

"Perfect!" Andrew relieved Chloe of their son, and then took Samantha's hand to lead them back to the nursery for a tea party.

Chloe smiled after them and then turned to her sister. "Well, shall we prepare for this evening?"

~*~

Andrew Wetherby walked into the parlor of Ashbury Manor, where his closest family members and family friends were making merry. Chloe and the children were already there as well. Samantha had found her cousins and now played with them on the rug before the great fire. His brothers-in-law, Steven and James Hawthorne, stood by the sidebar, which was stocked with fine scotch and brandy. And Chloe's sister, Cassandra, clung to her side, clearly unsure, at the ripe age of twelve, whether she should be playing with the children or conversing with the adults.

He watched Chloe intently as he leaned against the doorjamb, wondering if she was all right. It wasn't any secret that she was a bit nervous about her cousin's return, despite the fact they'd visited them in Scotland. Still, it had been a long time since then. And Andrew would be lying if he said he wasn't a bit nervous himself. He'd spent a long time engaged to Elizabeth, and the fact that she married his brother could make for an awkward family gathering. Could four years really make them all forget what had happened?

Voices from the front hall brought him from his thoughts and sent his nerves skittering to his extremities. They would find out soon enough just how awkward this holiday would be.

Andrew stepped out into the corridor and waited for Michael and Elizabeth to make their way towards him. As they did, one thing became very apparent. He smiled widely at his brother and sister-in-law, and they both beamed back at him. His nerves melted away as he kissed Elizabeth on her cheek and then embraced his twin. It had been far too long.

"Oh, heavens," Elizabeth said, as she stood by watching them. "I never expected to be so emotional, but this reunion..."

"Lizzie!"

Andrew and Michael stepped aside to allow Chloe into the corridor. She ran to Elizabeth and gathered her in her arms as both women dissolved into tears.

Katherine & William

Katherine, Duchess of Weston, didn't care how long it had been since everyone had seen one another, there wouldn't be any tears at her party. So when she saw her sisters-in-law blubbering in the corridor outside the drawing room, she knew she must put a stop to it.

"Ladies, you're going to make a mess for Sturgeon to clean up," she said as she approached the little group of sappy relatives. "Come now, it's Christmas. Let us put smiles on our faces and rejoice that we are once again together."

"So wonderful to see you, too, sister dear." Her little brother Michael said, though in all honesty, he wasn't little at all. As a matter of fact, Katherine was rather dwarfed next to her brothers, blast them.

"Don't be cross with me, Michael," she said, moving in for a hug and a kiss from him. "I'm simply trying to be a good hostess."

"You are the very the best, Kat. Never doubt it."

She smiled widely at her brother. "You've always been my favorite, you know?"

"Pardon me?" Andrew stepped forward, looking affronted. "Isn't that what you said to me just last week when I brought you all those fashion plates from Mother?"

Katherine gave Andrew her most placating smile and kissed him on the cheek just as Sturgeon rang the dinner bell. "Wonderful! Just wait until you see the dinner buffet—I've been planning it ever since I learned Michael and Lizzie were coming home for Christmas."

Katherine relished hosting this Christmas Eve dinner, and the fact that she'd succeeded in bringing everyone home for it. It was a rare thing to have all of them in one place at one time, what with everyone being scattered all over Scotland and England.

Her heart gave a little flutter as her husband took her arm and led her the rest of the way to the dining room.

"You've done a magnificent job of putting this together, my darling," William purred close to her ear. "You are one extraordinary woman."

After four children, it was a wonder that he still made her heart beat so quickly and her palms go a little sweaty. He was quite the most incredible and handsome man she'd ever known, with his wavy blond locks and blue eyes that always seemed to know just what she was thinking.

"You're thinking about last night, aren't you?" he asked, a mischievous gleam in those azure eyes.

Katherine's skin heated at the memory of their passionate evening together...and morning, if truth be told. Something about the holidays made her rather wanton, it seemed.

"You are very naughty," she whispered, "talking of such things *now*."

"My deepest apologies, but truly, I can't think of anything I'd rather talk about."

Katherine giggled and swatted her husband on the arm as they arrived at the door to the dining room. She took stock of her work as they passed over the threshold and smiled triumphantly. The dining room was a masterpiece. She'd had the walls repapered in red damask and hung garlands everywhere that would allow for them. Red velvet curtains framed the windows, through which they could watch the light snow that fell on the other side. All the Argand lamps that usually lit the dining room had been removed in favor of simple candlelight, and the room positively glowed with the romance of the holiday.

At her cue, the maid in charge of the small orchestra she'd hired for the evening scurried from the room. Only moments later, the sounds of Corelli's Christmas Concerto wafted from the music room. It was just loud enough to be heard, but not so loud they couldn't enjoy stimulating conversation around the dinner table.

"Brava, sister," Benjamin said as he planted a kiss to her cheek. "Christmas has never been so perfect."

"You always know just the right thing to say to me, don't you?" she teased her elder brother.

"Woe to the man who doesn't," William chimed in.

Normally, Katherine might have taken offense to their jesting, but her mood was far too sunny tonight, so she laughed along with them as she strode to the far end of the table to take her seat.

~*~

Standing opposite his wife at the far end of the long table, William Hart, Duke of Weston, couldn't help but smile. Though he hoped his mother-in-law's demise wouldn't be for a good many years, he knew his Katherine would be a brilliant matriarch for this burgeoning family in years to come. Not only was she beautiful with her near-black hair and olive skin, but she was regal, in a way that only someone born and bred to this life could be.

And while she could often be a bit overbearing, there wasn't a person alive who could do what she did. The Christmas banquet was only one small aspect of what she was capable of. The bigger of her accomplishments was in bringing the entire family together for the event, including his little brother, Wesley. Though calling him a little brother was a bit out of line, wasn't it? He was grown now, married to Faith exactly seven years tomorrow, with a family of his own. Quite a large one at that, with three already and one on the way.

Dinner, as was always the case with this family, was a lively affair. The Wetherby siblings still needled one another as if they were children, and everyone else laughed at the repartee. William's heart swelled with gratitude as he looked up and down the long table. How far they had come from that Christmas seven years ago, trapped by the snow in their home in the Lake District. Katherine had been so very disappointed that her party had been ruined and that she wouldn't have her family with her for the holiday. William's heart constricted just thinking about the stricken look on her face when she realized no one could get through the snow.

Of course, orchestrating the wedding of Wesley and Faith had taken some of the sting out of the disappointing circumstances.

But now here they were, a large, lively family, all in a good health, all seemingly happy. Many often thought the accomplishments of a duke were measured in land and holdings, but William didn't care about any of that. What he cared about were the people at this table. The people he called family.

Elizabeth & Chloe

Lizzie looked up from her spot behind the pianoforte to find her cousin coming towards her. They'd yet to have a moment alone since her arrival, and she couldn't wait to catch up with Chloe. Her dear cousin had aged in the past four years. Not that she looked old, but...mature. Her wild, red hair was contained in a soft chignon, and the corners of her eyes and mouth proved that she'd laughed and smiled a great deal in the last few years. That made Lizzie exceedingly happy. After all Chloe had been through, it seemed she'd finally found her happily ever after. What Chloe didn't know—what she seemed uncertain of—was whether or not Lizzie had also found her happily ever after.

"Elizabeth," she said as she approached, warmth and love in her tone and in her beaming smile. She reached out and Lizzie turned on the bench to take her hands.

"Do you think anyone will miss us if we steal away to the library for a few minutes?" Lizzie asked.

"The children are abed and the men..." They both turned their gazes to the sitting area on the other side of the room where the men laughed and drank before the fire. "Well, I think it will be all right."

Lizzie followed her cousin down the corridor of Ashbury Manor. The familiar walls brought a warmth to her belly and smile to her lips. She'd spent many an afternoon having tea with her future sisters-in-law here. Of course, that was when she thought she was marrying Andrew.

They slipped into the warmth of the library, with its blazing fire, glowing sconces and cozy sitting area. Lizzie plopped onto the settee next to her cousin and they both tucked their legs up under themselves, as if they were young girls, eager for gossip.

Chloe reached out and grabbed Lizzie's hands. "Now tell me, dear cousin. What have you been up to these four years?"

Lizzie laughed. "I've written you weekly, Chloe! You know everything."

"Yes, I know the details of your life at Dunbocan...but I don't know if you're happy. Or if you're still cross with Andrew and me. Please, tell me. Do you harbor ill feelings towards us?"

"The truth is," Lizzie began, "I was furious. I tortured Michael for months. I wanted him to pay dearly for what he'd done. I wanted to make him as miserable as I was."

"According to Michael's letters to Andrew, I believe you succeeded."

Lizzie couldn't stop the sly smile that came to her lips as she thought back on her antics. "Well, I suppose I took it a tad far when I threw the candlestick at his head. I was fortunate my aim was off, and that he had the good sense to duck out of the way. I never would have forgiven myself had I caused permanent damage to that beautiful face."

"It *is* magnificent, isn't it?" Chloe added with a wink. Being married to twins with identical features was a funny thing, that.

"But the truth is, he never stopped believing in me. Or perhaps it was his own self he believed in so strongly. That we were meant to be. That our marriage could be a happy one if only he could break down the walls I'd built around myself."

"And was he right?"

Lizzie nodded. "More right than I ever could have imagined. Oh, Chloe, I've changed so much. I'm not at all the gregarious, frivolous, silly girl I once was. And I feel just horrible for all that I put you through when you came to be my chaperone."

"Nonsense!" Chloe stopped her, squeezing her hands tighter. "You were just what I needed. You got me out of those dreadful black dresses. You made me realize that there was life after Sam—that I could be *happy*."

"Perhaps," Lizzie agreed. "But I could have been gentler and more thoughtful about it."

Chloe shrugged. "Perhaps. But let us put all past events aside, shall we?"

"Oh, Chloe, I have missed you so." Tears sprang to Lizzie's eyes, the emotion of the moment coming over her without notice. How could such a tiny thing inside of her cause so much commotion all the time? Lizzie was certain she had cried more in the last six months than she'd done in her entire life.

"Please don't cry, dear cousin." Chloe moved closer and put her arms around Lizzie. "We are together again, both exceedingly happy...and here you are, burgeoning with child."

Silence fell over them, the only sound Lizzie's sniffling.

Finally, Lizzie spoke. "That has been the hardest road of all." Her heart twisted, thinking back on all the babies she'd lost over the last four years. All the pain she'd suffered, both physically and emotionally, waiting for God to grant her a healthy pregnancy.

Chloe squeezed her hands. "I wish I could have been there for you."

"You were," Lizzie assured her. "Your letters were such a great comfort to me."

Chloe smiled. "I'm glad for that."

"Chloe!"

"Beth!"

The sounds of their husband's voices, almost as identical as their looks, resounded in the corridor outside the library. Both women jumped from their seats and rushed to meet their husbands at the door.

"What is it, Michael?" Lizzie asked.

Michael reached out a hand to his wife, as Andrew did the same to Chloe.

"Come," Andrew said, tugging her down the corridor. "There is a surprise."

The four of them rushed toward the foyer of the townhouse, where the rest of the family had gathered at the open door. Voices wafted in from the outside, a chorus of *Here We Come a-Wassailing*, lilting on the air.

Chloe nuzzled between Katherine and Benjamin to see over the heads of her nieces and nephews who stood on the porch, a light dusting of snow sprinkling onto their precious little heads.

At the front of the group of carolers stood her sister, Grace, her husband, the Duke of Somerset, beside her. The duke's sister Hannah and her new husband Dr. Alcott, stood on the other side, with his sister and brother-in-law, Lord and Lady Wolverton. Even the curmudgeonly Dowager Duchess of Somerset sang out into the cold. Behind all of them stood at least twenty other women, all beaming with pride. They were the women of Hannah's Home—the charitable organization Hannah had begun to help women of ill repute turn their lives around. It was still in the early stages, but Chloe could already see that it was going to make a huge difference in the lives of these women.

Standing there in the cold, surrounded by family, Chloe had never felt so warm.

Evan & Grace

"We wish you a Merry Christmas, and a Happy New Year!" Grace, Duchess of Somerset, sang out as loudly as she could, even though she knew she had quite a horrible voice. Singing had never been her forte, and yet, she couldn't hold back. Not tonight. Not when so much joy and happiness filled her heart.

Evan squeezed her hand, and she glanced over at him as the group began a rousing rendition of *Joy to the World*. He was smiling just as widely as she was, and so was his mother, for that matter. A Christmas miracle, for sure.

Hannah and Graham, who ought to have been enjoying their wedding night, sang out loudly as well. It seemed the Christmas Spirit was with them all this evening.

As the song came to a close, the Duchess of Hart pushed through the cheering children and insisted that everyone come inside for wassail and gingerbread. No one was inclined to say no to Her Grace, so they all filed into the warmth of the townhouse.

Grace sought out her sister first, enveloping her in a hug that might have said they hadn't seen one another in years, when really, they'd just been together earlier that day. Lizzie, however...

"Oh, Lizzie," Grace said, tears welling up in her throat. "It has been far too long."

"I couldn't agree more," her cousin said as they squeezed one another tightly. "I promise not to stay away so long next time."

"And I promise to come visit you in the Highlands. Evan will be more than glad to get away from London after the ordeal we've all been through with Beeston."

"Chloe only hinted at the situation in her letters. Come, let us settle in for tea and you can tell me the rest."

~*~

Evan watched as his wife walked away, her sister on one arm, her long-lost cousin on the other, a smile as wide as the Thames across her face. She was a happy little thing usually, but now, with a babe in her belly, with Hannah safe and happily wed, and with her cousin back home, well...he'd never seen her quite so content.

"You'll create horrible wrinkles smiling like that." His mother appeared beside him, the smile on her own face stealing any sting from her words.

"And I won't regret a one of them," he replied. "It is nice to see you smiling, Mother."

"Yes, well, I figured it was about time. Seventy years is a long time to hold one's face in a perpetual frown."

"I'm sorry your life was not worth smiling about," Evan said, and he meant it. He knew what it was to be unhappy, and he didn't wish it on anyone.

But the dowager only smiled wider. "There is nothing to be sorry about, my son." She shrugged. "So it took me a little longer to find happiness...at least I found it before I died."

Evan gave a little chuckle. "Indeed. Come," he said, proffering his arm for his mother, "let us get a glass of wassail."

Hannah & Graham

In spite of the cold weather, Hannah couldn't help but want to be outside in the falling snow. It was quite magical, and she didn't want to miss a minute of it. Besides, it was getting rather warm in the house with so many crowded into the drawing room now. But she'd not complain—it was quite generous of the duchess to open her home to them on Christmas Eve.

Hannah wrapped her arms around herself as she stepped onto the terrace and looked up into the waning moon and falling snow. She closed her eyes and let the cold flakes trickle onto her face and all the joy and gratitude of the season wash over her.

"I thought I'd find you here," came a deep voice as a pair of strong arms snaked about her waist.

She giggled. "I was hoping you would come looking for me. Isn't it romantic?"

"The *most* romantic," he replied, turning her around to face him.

She looked up into his eyes, so warm and full of love— love just for her. "I love you, Dr. Alcott," she said.

"And I love you, *Mrs. Alcott.*"

Hannah beamed. Oh, how wonderful not to be Lady Beeston anymore!

"But I do have one question that I've been meaning to ask you," he went on.

"Oh?"

"What in the world were you planning to do with all those women?"

Hannah laughed. "Oh, we had quite the elaborate plan, actually. It involved lots of rope and a ship bound for Jamaica."

Graham threw back his head. "I'm quite sorry you never got to see it through."

"I'm not," Hannah replied, and she meant it. "Then he might still be alive, and I'd always be looking over my shoulder. I will owe a great debt to Miss Delaney for as long as I live."

"I'm just glad no one went to Newgate."

"Aren't we all?"

Graham leaned down and captured Hannah's lips in a searing kiss. "Do you think we could sneak away early?"

Hannah grinned at him as parts of her began to heat. "It *is* our wedding night, after all. I can't imagine anyone would fault us."

"Well, then," he scooped her into his arms. "Let us make our escape."

Hannah giggled all the way through the garden and as they made their way around the front of the house to where the coaches awaited their owners. As they climbed aboard Graham's carriage, there was a bit of excitement at the front door. Hannah didn't recognize the young man standing there, but apparently, his presence was most welcome.

"Take us home, John!" Graham called, and then he climbed in and away they went.

Becky & Stephen

"Becky! Come quickly!"

Becky, Viscountess Hastings, turned away from her conversation to the sound of Phoebe's voice in the foyer. "What on earth?" she muttered to her husband, who stood beside her.

Stephen, her proud and handsome viscount, shrugged, his brandy sloshing gently in his glass as he did so. "Sounds rather urgent," he said. "I wouldn't keep her waiting."

Becky turned from the group and started toward the foyer when her niece, Lydia, bounced into view, her blonde curls shaking with her excitement.

"Lydia?" she said. "What is it?"

"Uncle!" she called into the drawing room. "You must come too!"

And then as Stephen approached, she grabbed them both by the hand and led them into the foyer. There, divesting himself of a snow-covered greatcoat, stood their nephew—who was truly more like their son—Max.

Becky could hardly believe her eyes. He hadn't been home in months, and had even written recently to inform them he'd not be able to join them for Christmas. And yet, here he was, flesh and blood, in the foyer of Ashbury Manor. He looked older, so mature, but there were still traces of the little boy he'd once been. The little boy that used to try to frighten her with frogs and snakes.

Lydia threw herself at him, and he squeezed back, lifting her so her feet came off the ground. They were everything to one another, having lost both their parents at such a young age. Sure, they had Stephen and Becky and their little cousins, but no one would ever understand the bond the two of them shared.

Becky glanced sideways at her husband. Stephen had always been the stoic, brooding type, but tonight, with the glimmer of tears in his eyes, he looked anything *but* stoic. And once Lydia was out of the way, he stepped forward to hug his nephew, unafraid of showing the boy just how happy he was to have him there.

"We thought you weren't coming," Becky said, stepping forward to accept her own hug from her nephew.

"Change of plans," Max said. "I couldn't stay away any longer."

Lydia sidled back up to him. He put his arm around her and kissed the top of her head. Goodness, when had *she* gotten so grown up? Only a few more years until she'd have her first season. It seemed impossible that the time had passed so quickly, but here they were. Older, wiser, and happier than they'd ever been.

"Where are my little cousins?" Max asked, his blue eyes bright, his cheeks still rosy from the cold.

"Already abed, I'm afraid," Becky replied. "But come, everyone else is in the parlor."

Phoebe & Benjamin

Phoebe, Marchioness of Eastleigh, stood at the edge of the drawing room near the hearth, her arms folded over her chest, a lump the size of Yorkshire in her throat. They were all here. Every last one of her beloved relations, and more. Everyone who mattered to her in this world was somehow crammed into this one drawing room, laughing, smiling, singing, embracing. It was the greatest gift she could have ever hoped for.

"Did your Christmas wish come true?" came her husband's voice from beside her. She glanced up at him, still as handsome as the day she'd met him all those years ago at the Stapleton Ball. And as kind and loving and generous as the day she'd married him. It hadn't been the easiest courtship, what with she and her mother all but in the poor house and him wrongly believing he had killed Phoebe's father, but Phoebe couldn't regret a single moment of it.

"I don't think I've ever been so happy in all my life," she replied.

Benjamin sidled up behind her and snaked his arms about her waist. "You were awfully happy evening last, if I remember right."

Phoebe threw back her head and laughed. "Indeed," she said, her cheeks heating at the memory. "Then I should say this has been the happiest twenty-four hours of my life."

Benjamin turned her in his arms and she gazed up into his dark, Wetherby-brown eyes. Her heart was so filled with love, she thought it might burst.

"I have a present for you," Benajamin said.

"Oh, Ben! We promised we wouldn't exchange gifts this year."

"Yes, but last time I made that promise, you still got me something. I won't be fooled again."

Phoebe laughed. But that pocket watch had been too exquisite to leave behind at the shop. "Well, this year I truly didn't get you anything."

"Then we'll be even," he replied, placing her hand on his arm and leading her out of the room, away from the bustle of the family.

They walked quietly down the corridor, through a series of rooms and doors, the laughter and chatter from the drawing room fading with every step, until they arrived at the music room, already ablaze with candles.

"What is this?" Phoebe asked, as Benjamin closed the door behind them.

"Come." He made his way to the pianoforte and sat down, patting the empty seat beside him.

"Oh, Benjamin, it's been ages since we've played that thing."

"Exactly." He gazed down at her as she took her place beside him. "Far too long since I've made music with my bride." He poised his fingers above the keys, glancing sideways at her. "Let us see if you remember this one."

He began to play a tune so familiar to her heart that it nearly took her breath away. It was the one they'd played together that fateful night they'd encountered one another in the Sheffield's music room. They were supposed to be *listening* to the music in the other room, but fate had brought them together in another way. A very special way.

And just as she'd done that night long ago, Phoebe reached her right hand up as Benjamin dropped his, and together they played — his left hand, her right hand, working in tandem. In perfect harmony and precision, reminding her once again that she had found her soul's match, the other half of her heart.

"Merry Christmas, my darling," Benjamin murmured in her ear over the lilting Mozart tune.

Phoebe smiled. "Merry Christmas, my love."

THE END

More titles from
Jerrica Knight-Catania

The Daring Debutantes
The Robber Bride
The Gypsy Bride
The Stage Bride

The Wetherby Brides
A Gentleman Never Tells
More than a Governess
The Wary Widow
The Bedeviled Bride
Temptation of the Duke
How to Care for a Lady

Christmas Warms the Harts
The Perfect Kiss

Jerrica Knight-Catania knew from an early age that she was destined for romance. She would spend hours as a young girl sitting in a chair by an open window, listening to the rain, and dreaming of the day Prince Charming would burst in and declare his undying love for her. But it wasn't until she was 28-years-old, exhausted of her life in the theater, that she turned her focus toward writing Regency Romance novels. All her dreaming paid off, and she now gets to relive those romantic scenes she'd dreamt up as a young girl as she commits them to paper. She lives in sunny Palm Beach with her real life Prince Charming, their Princess-in-training, and their fluffy pup, Pumpkin.

Visit Jerrica's official website to learn more about her other books, the Wetherby family and to see what's new in her writing world! www.jerricasplace.com

Made in the USA
Middletown, DE
10 September 2018